Gothic Fantasy Easter Coloring Book for Adults

Experience Designs of Dark Bunnies, Mysterious Springtime Landscapes and Unique Egg Decorations, Ideal for Stress Relief & Relaxation

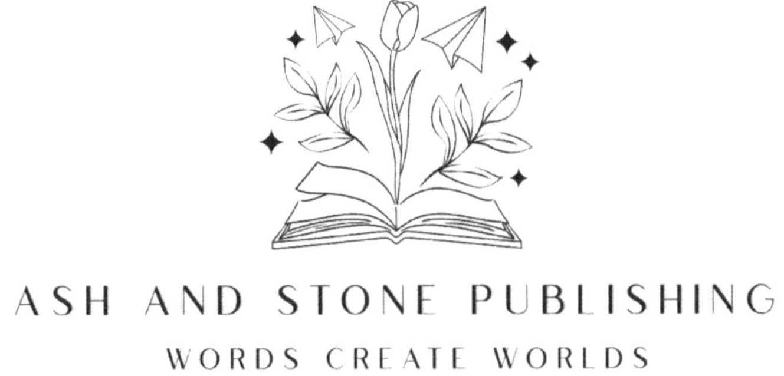

ASH AND STONE PUBLISHING

WORDS CREATE WORLDS

This Book Belongs To:

____

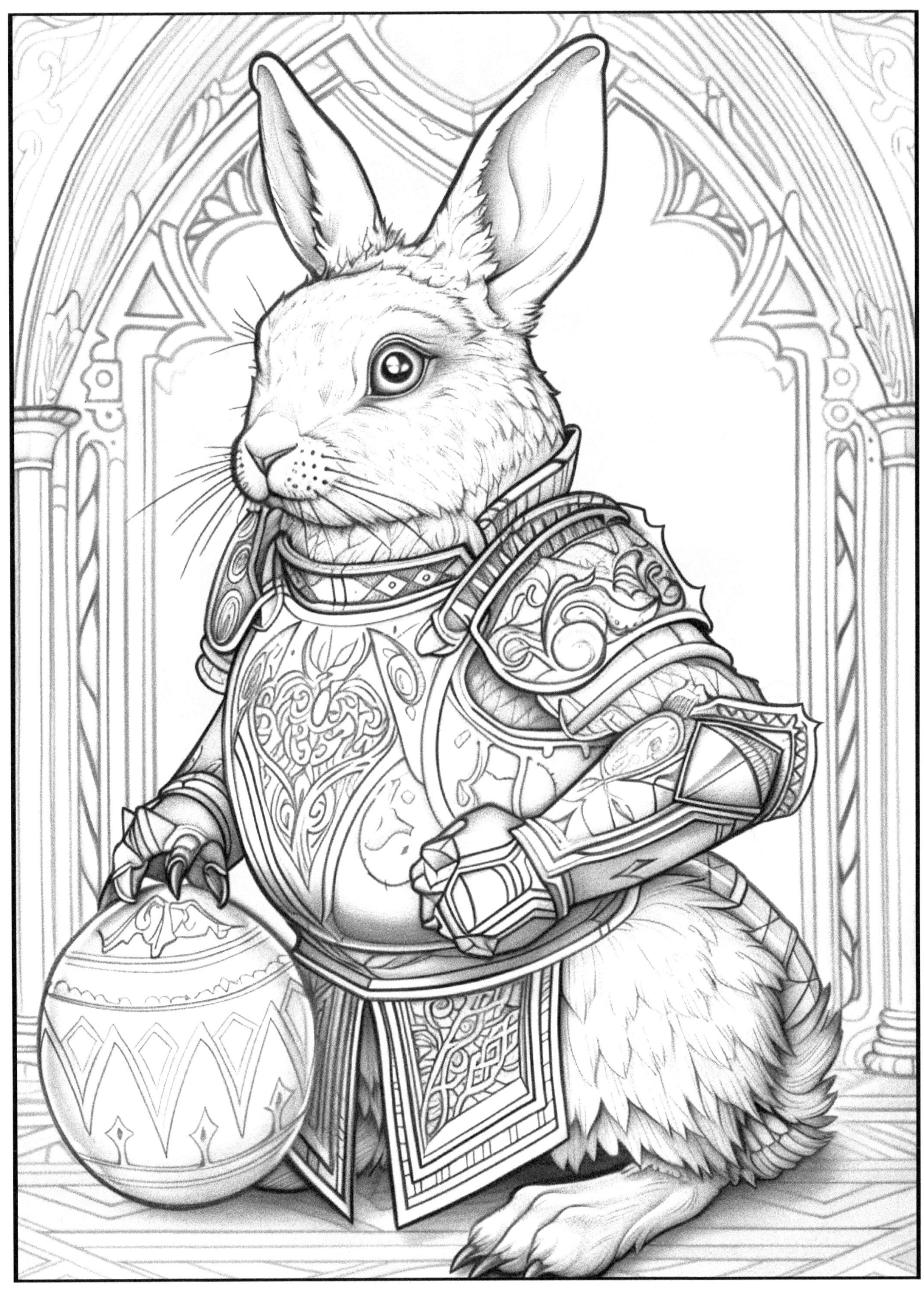

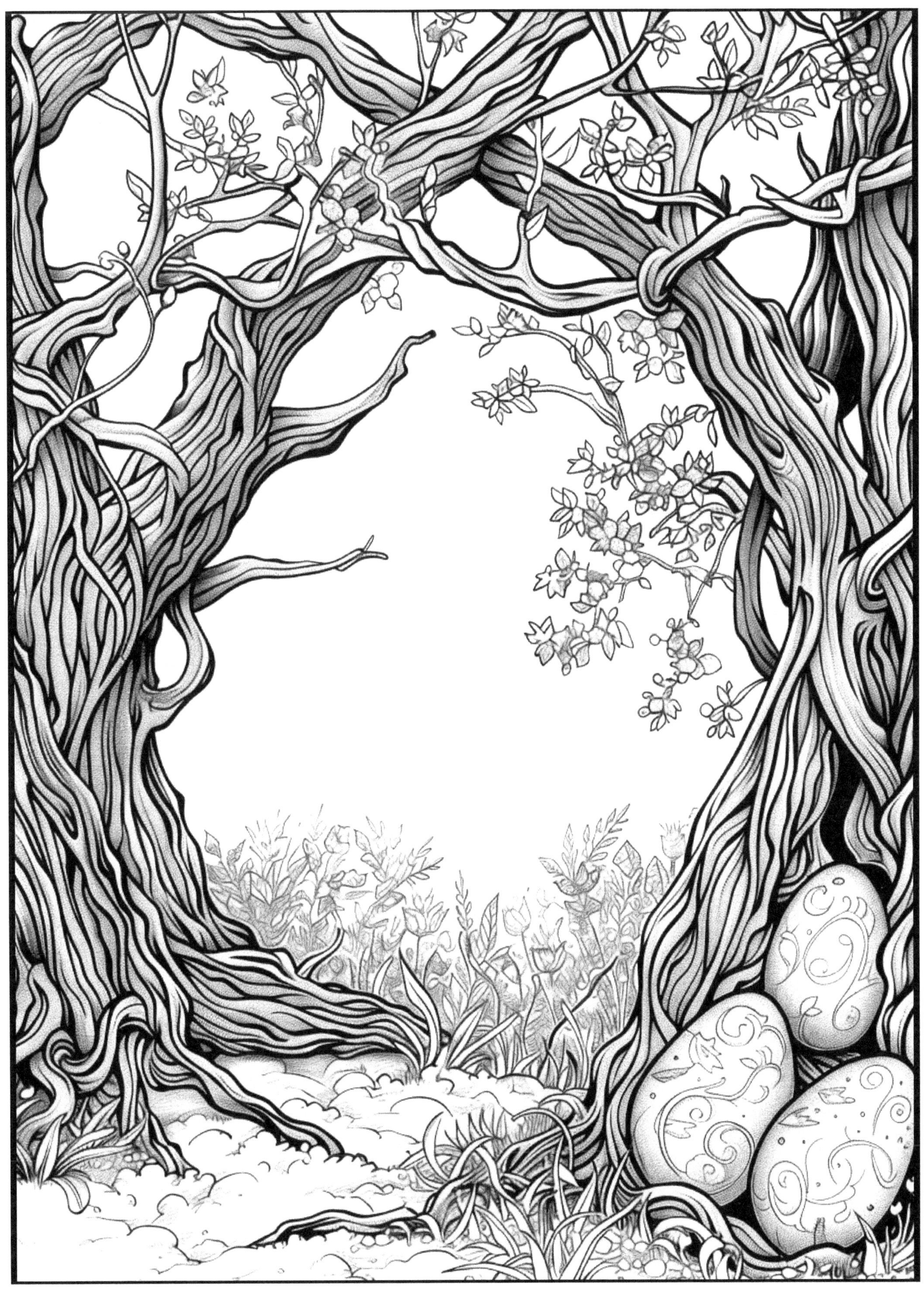

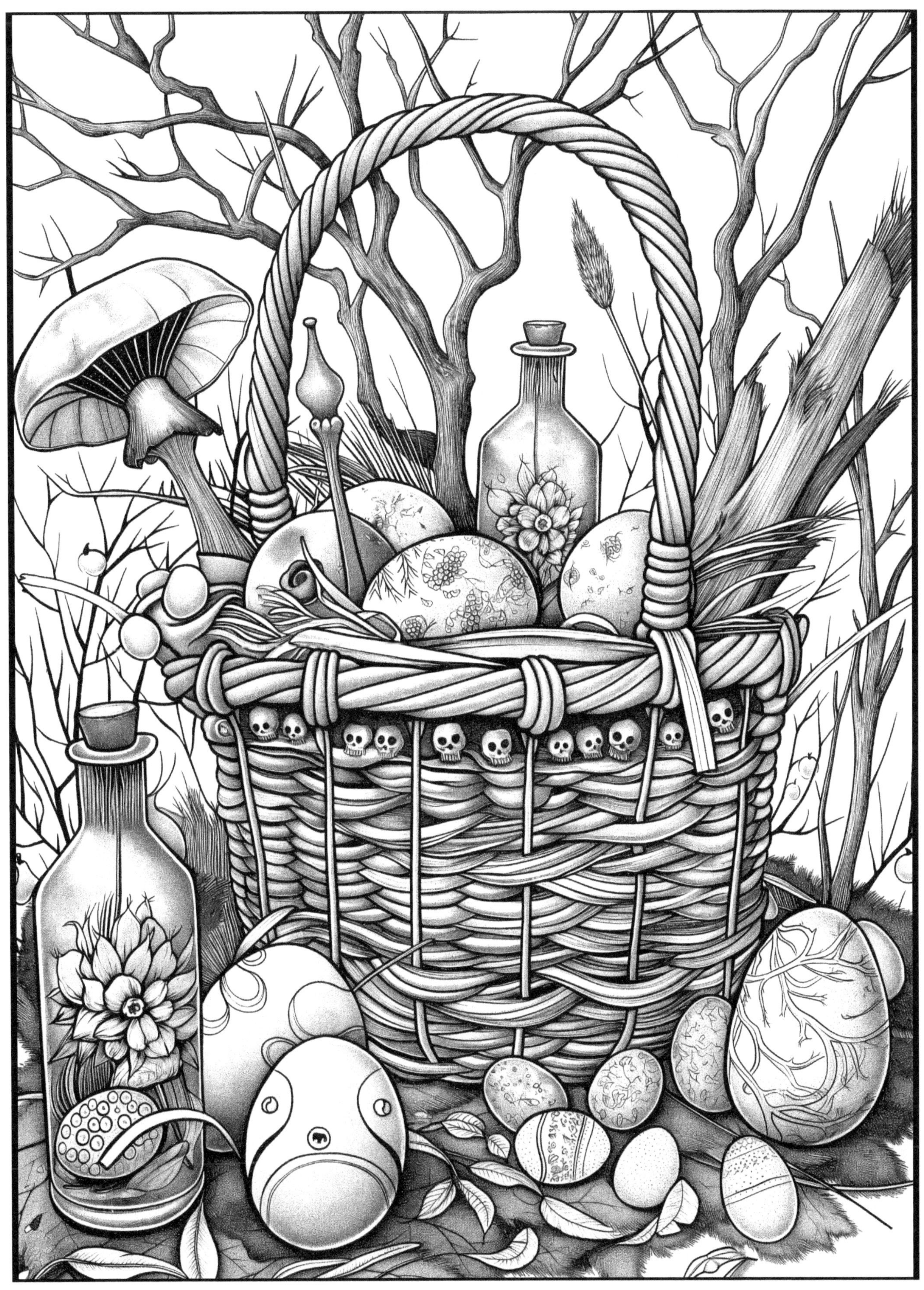

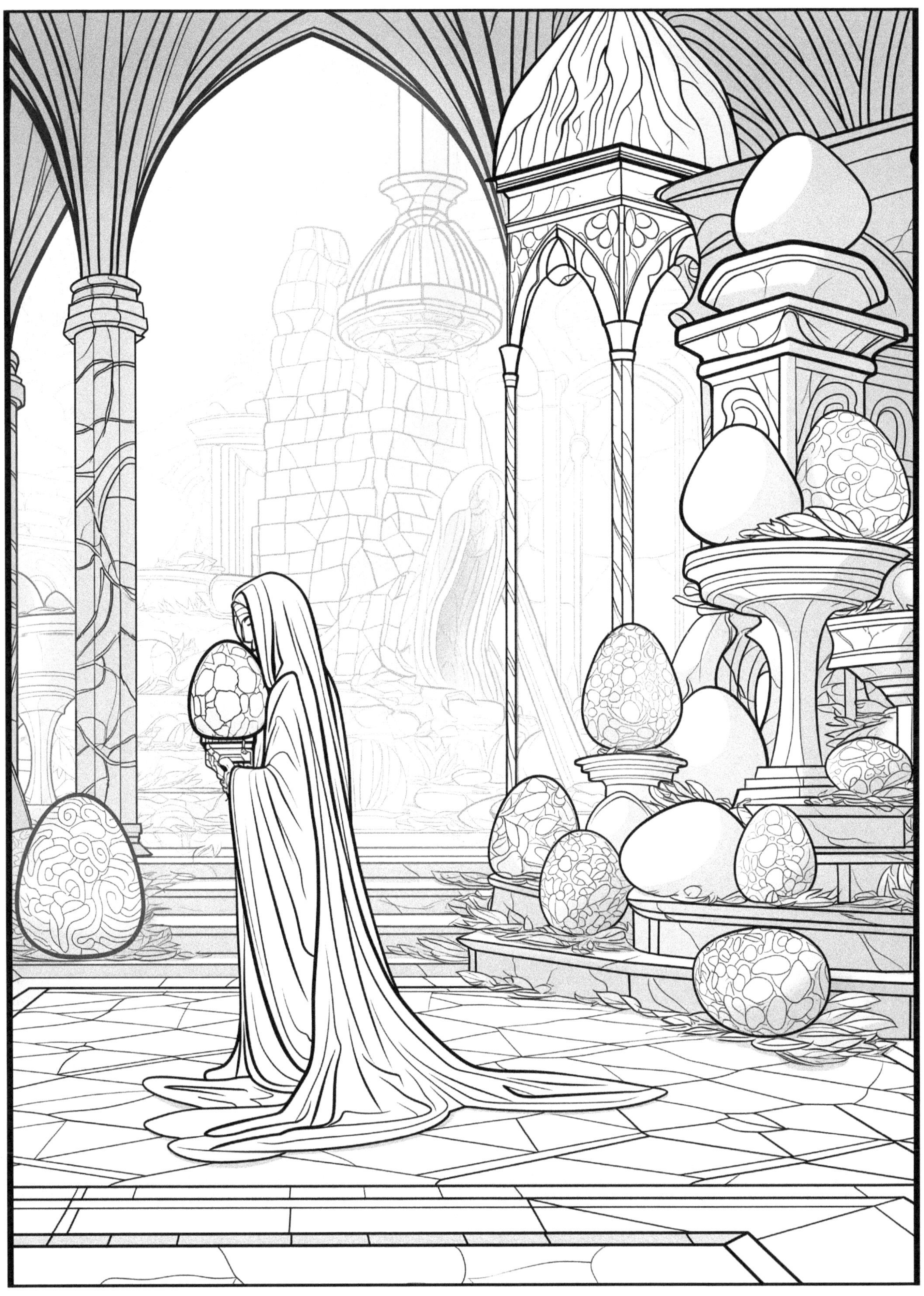

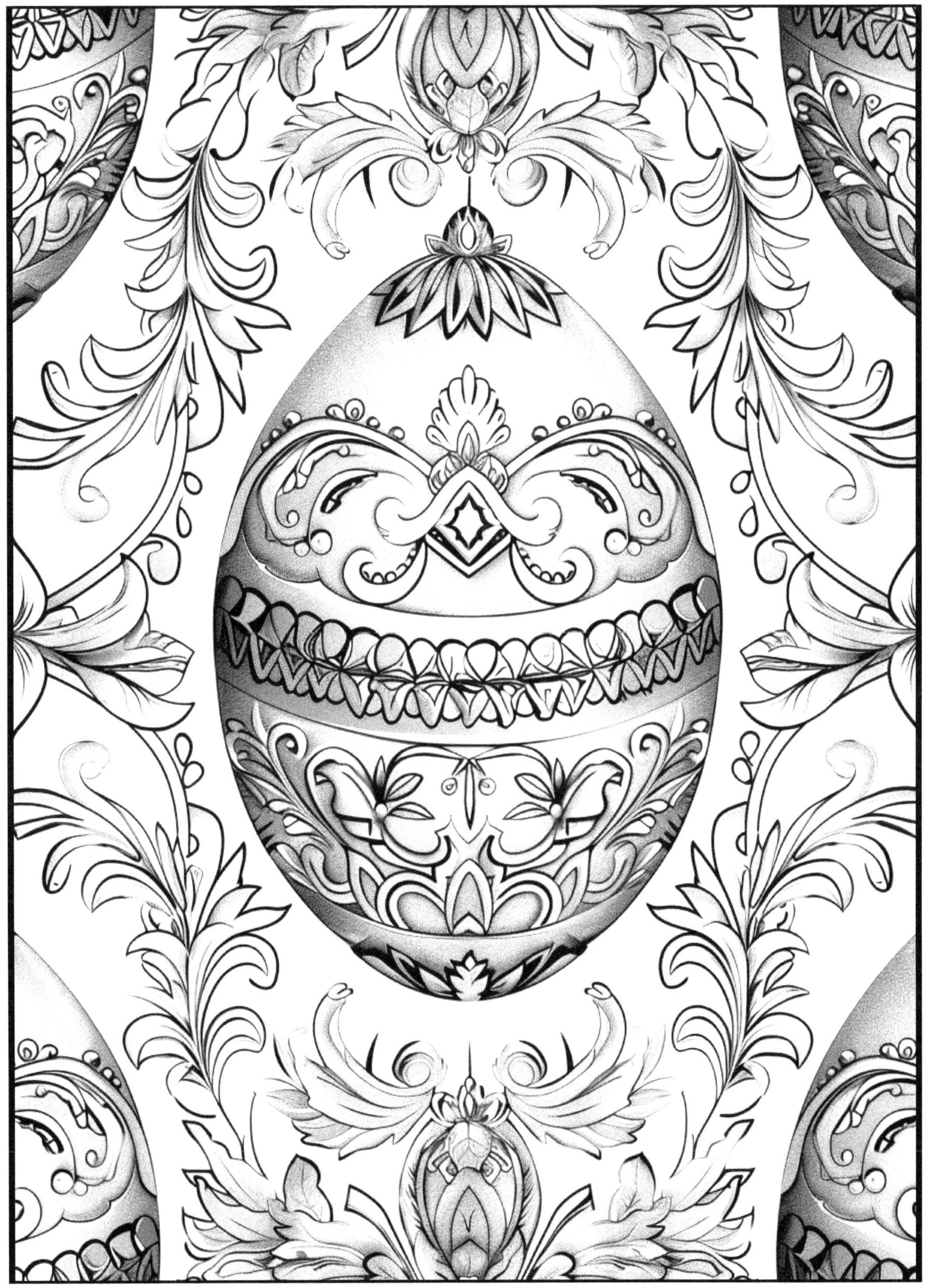

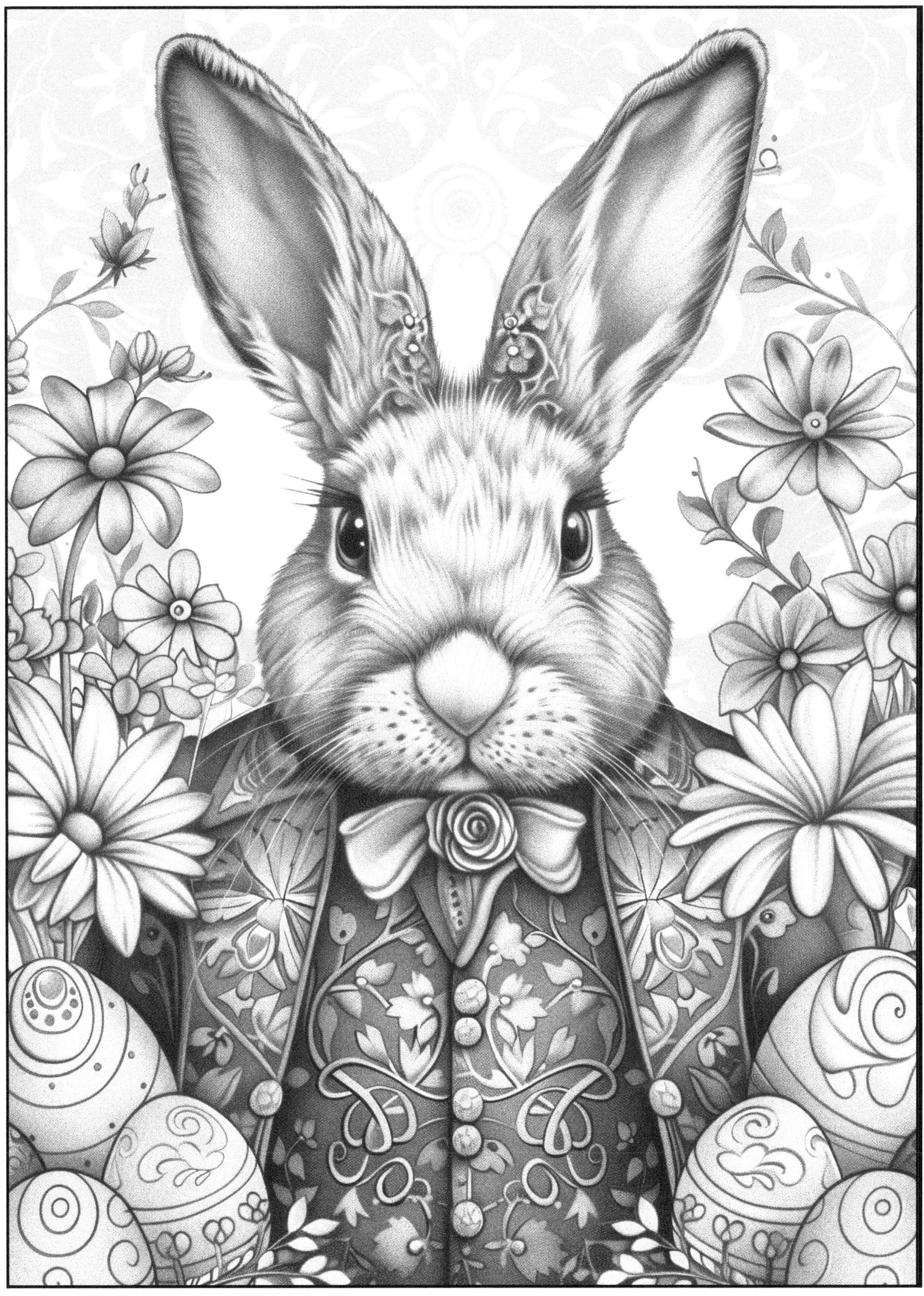

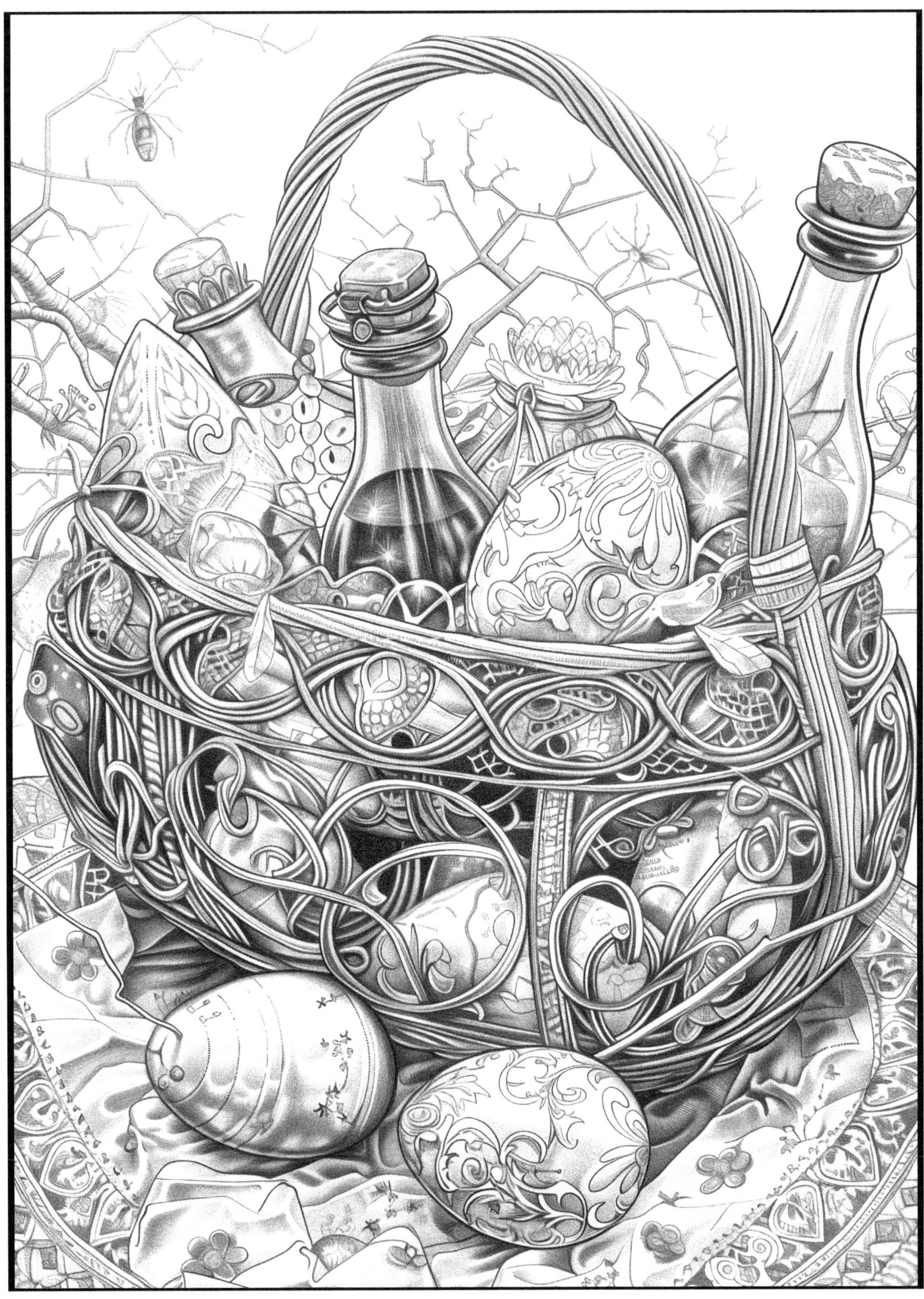

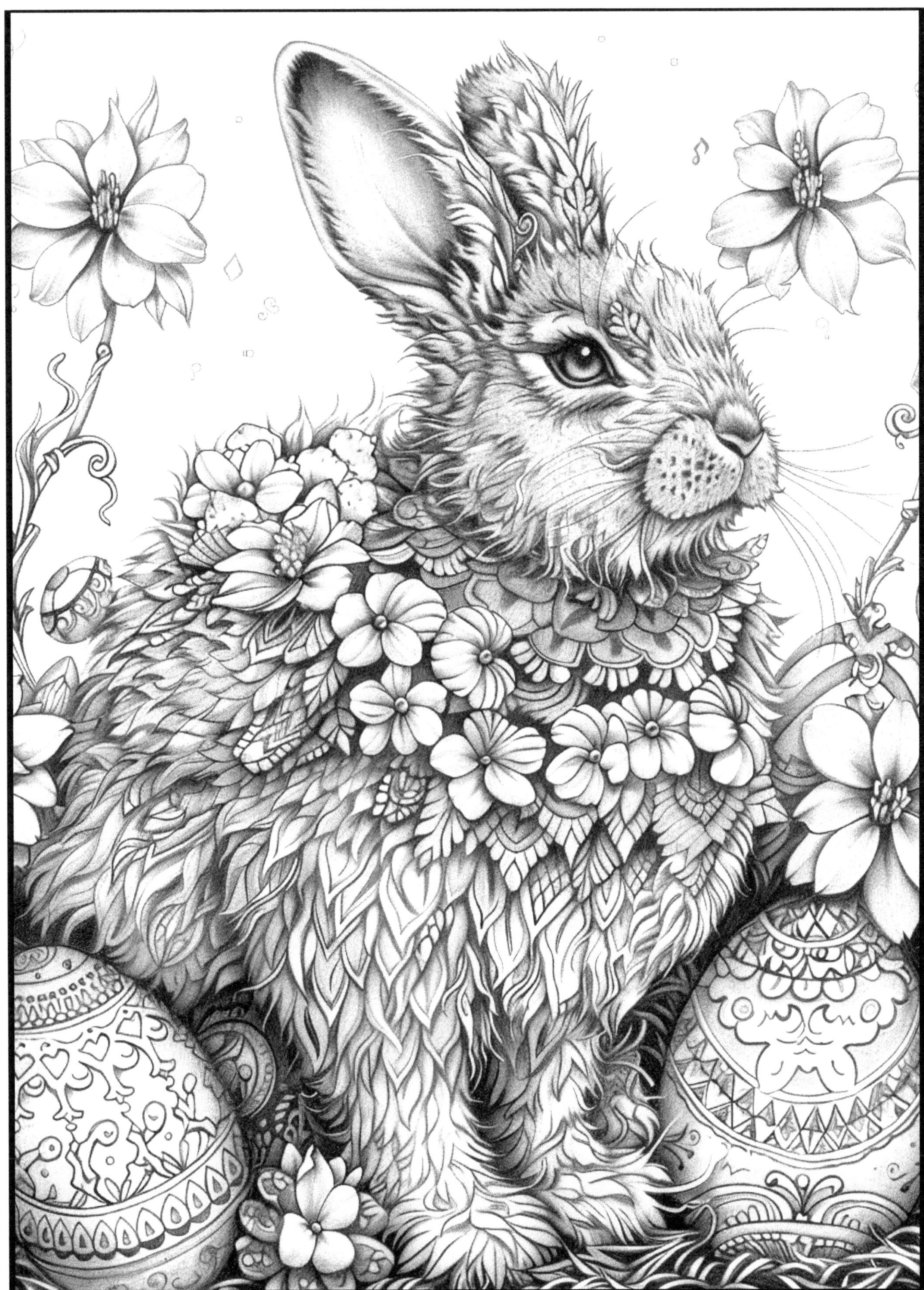

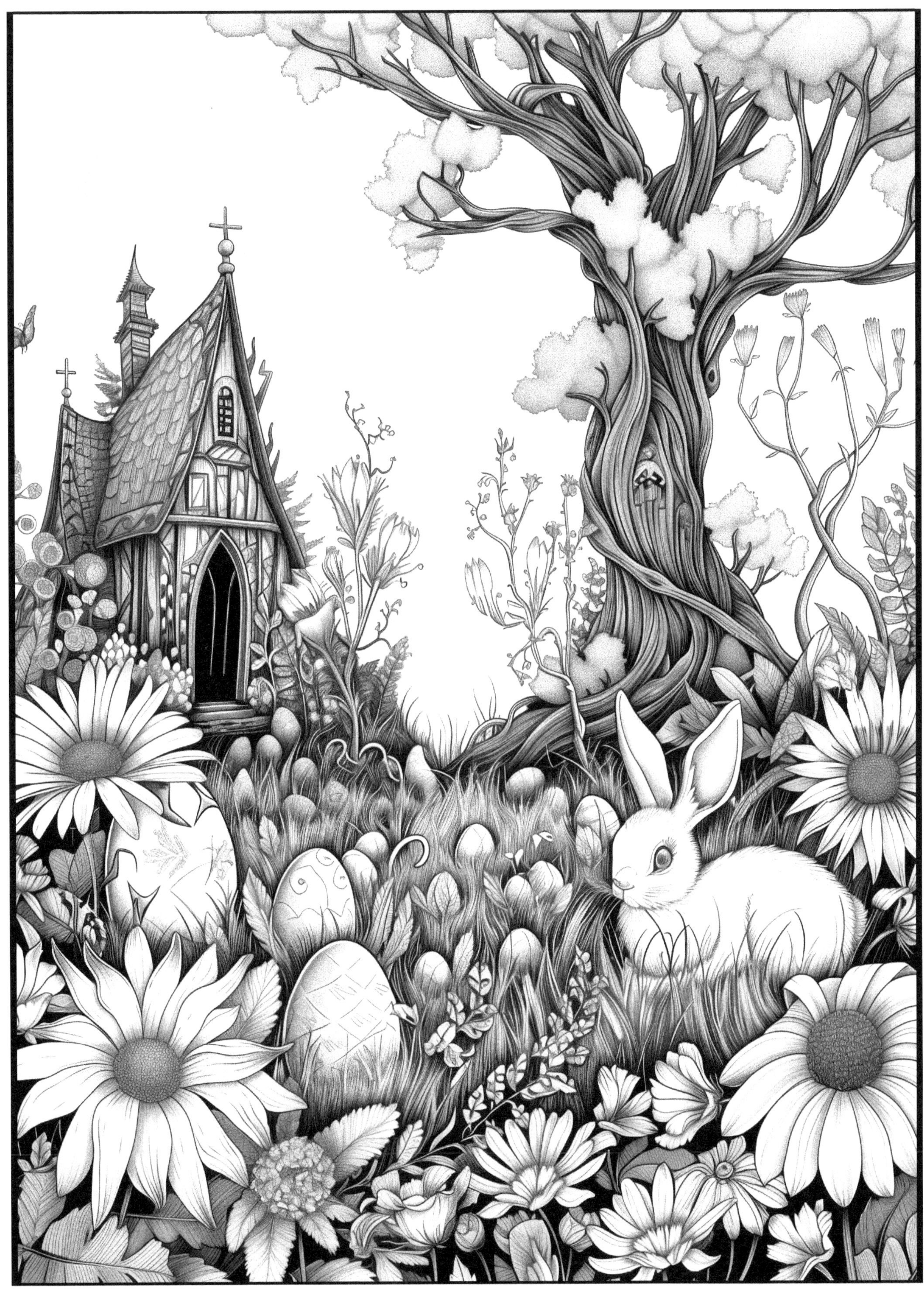

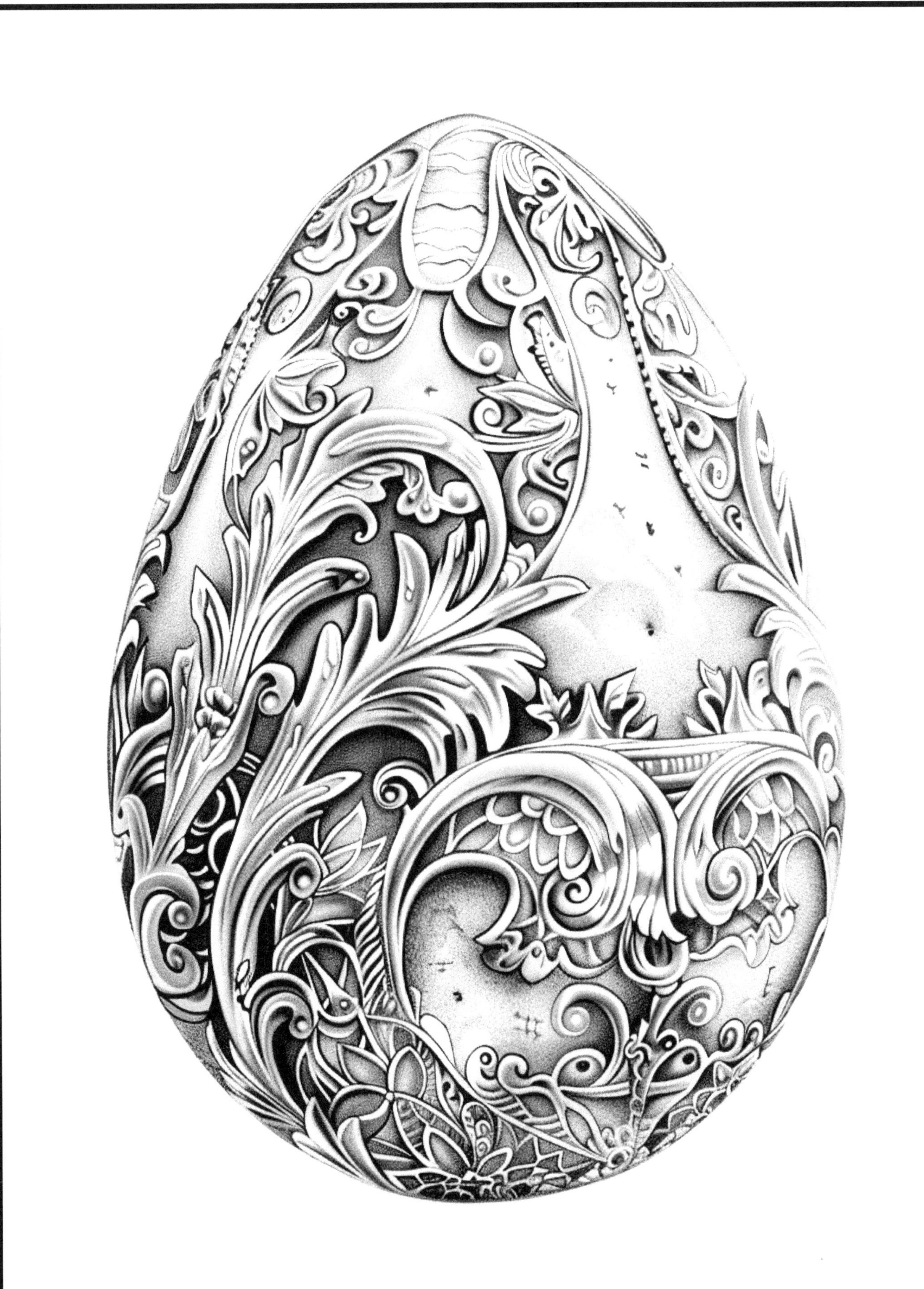

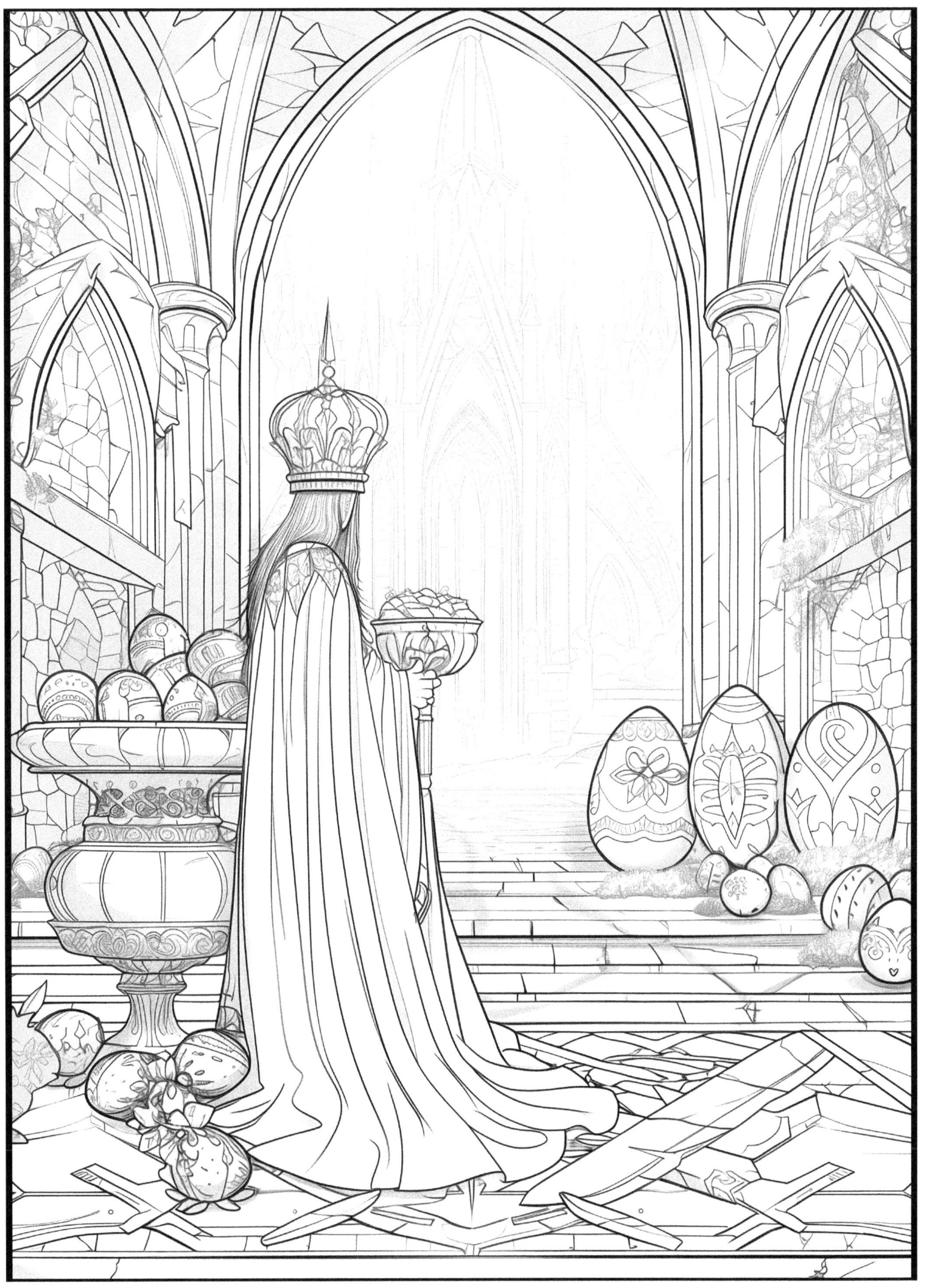

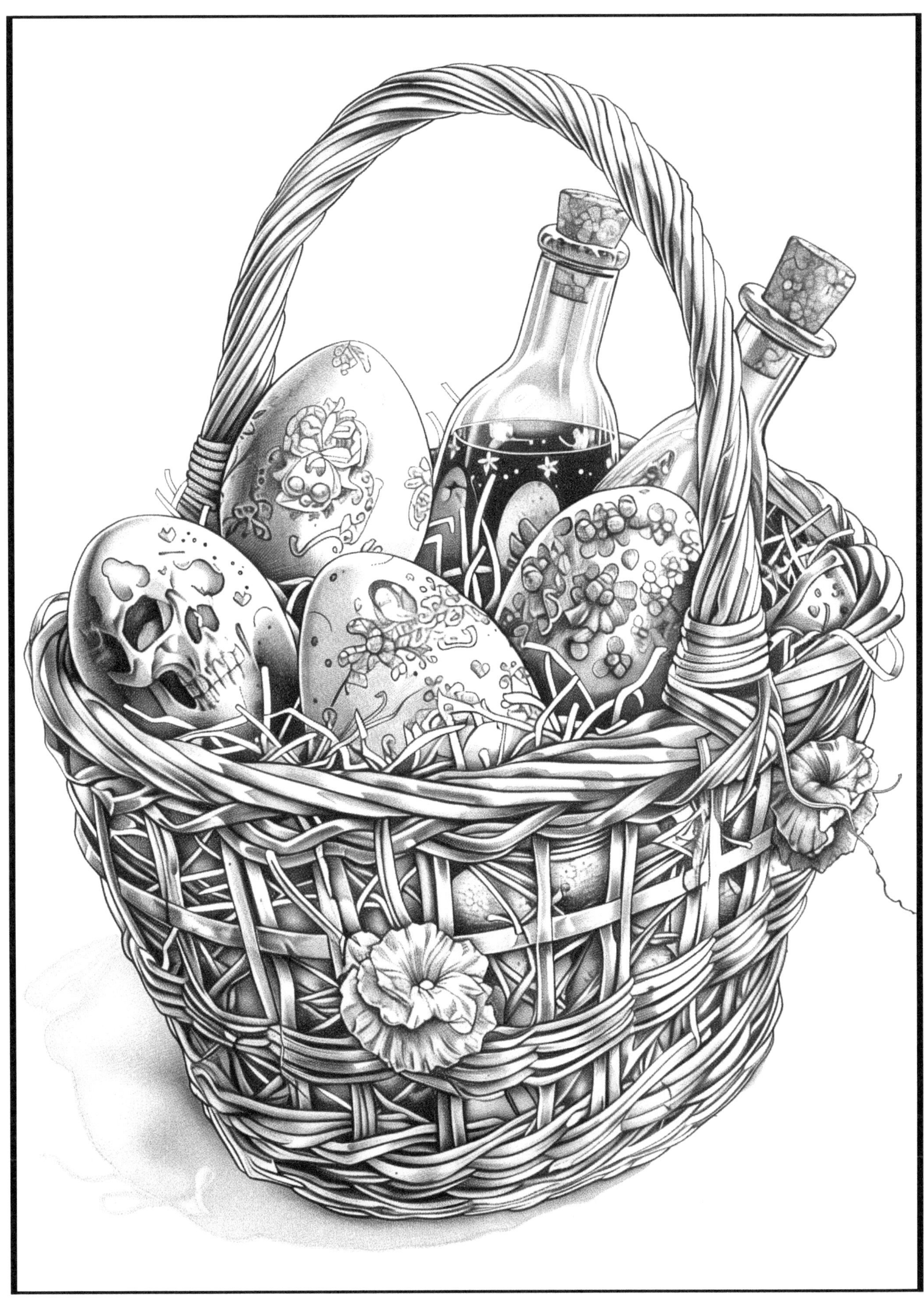

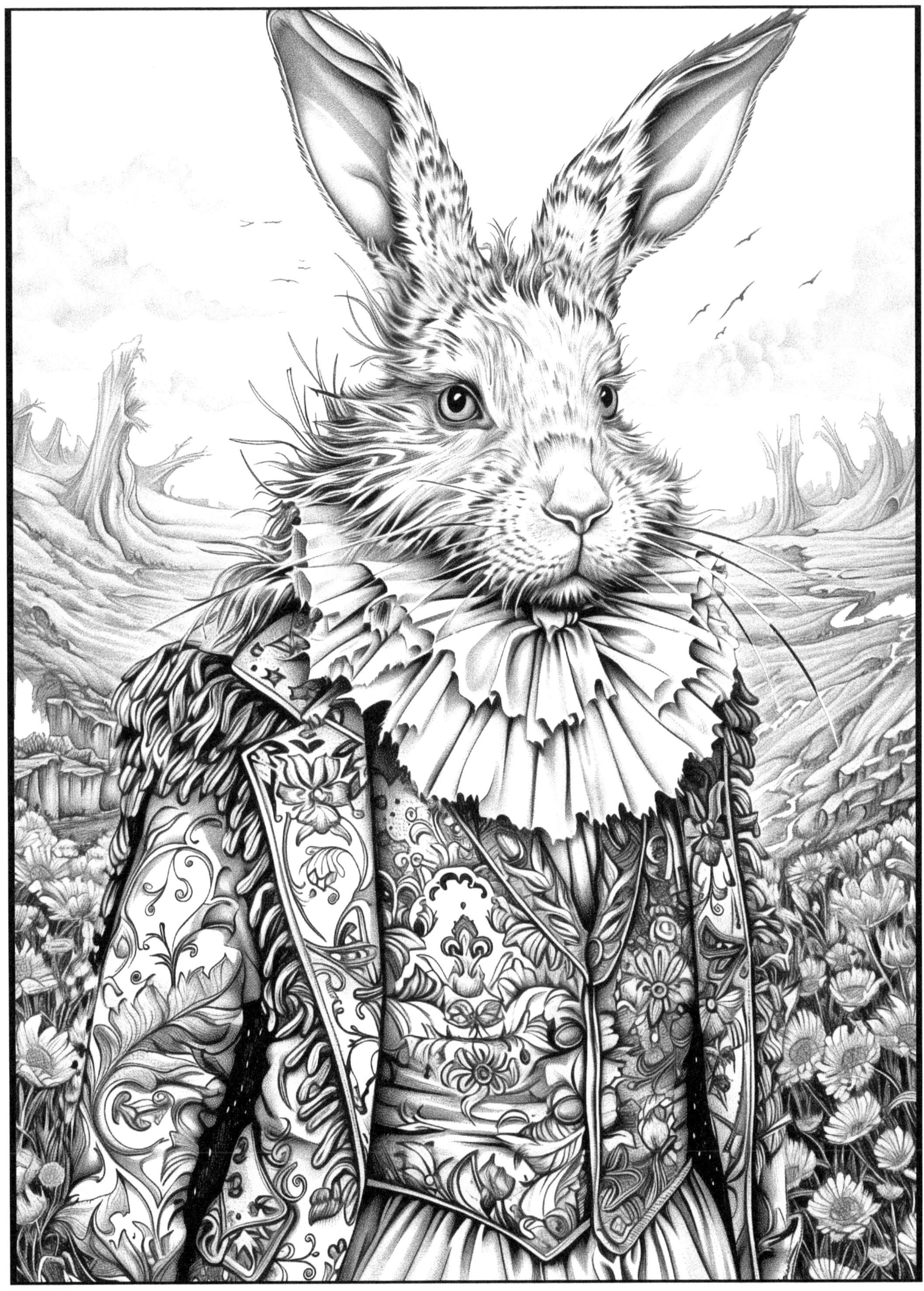

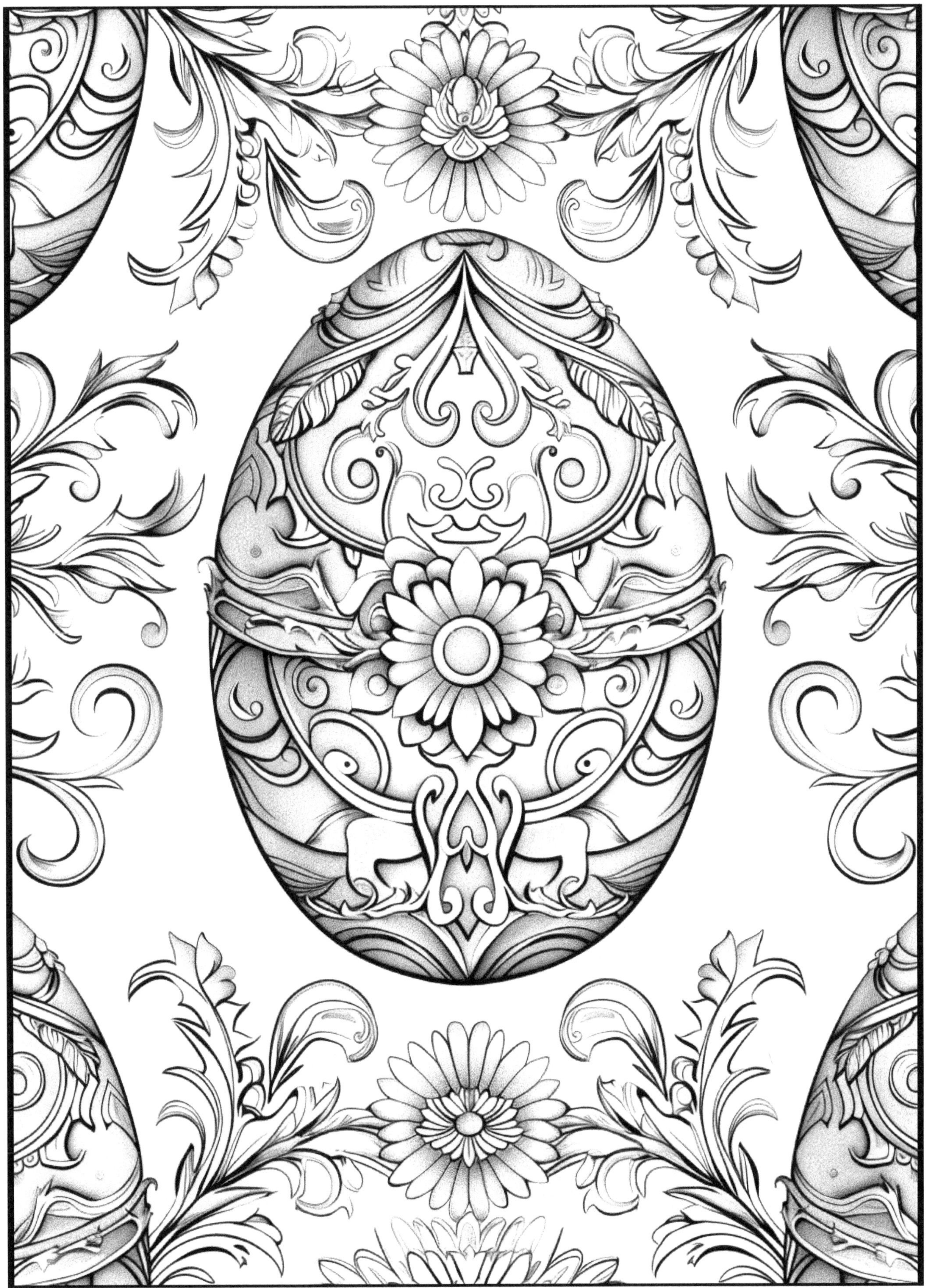

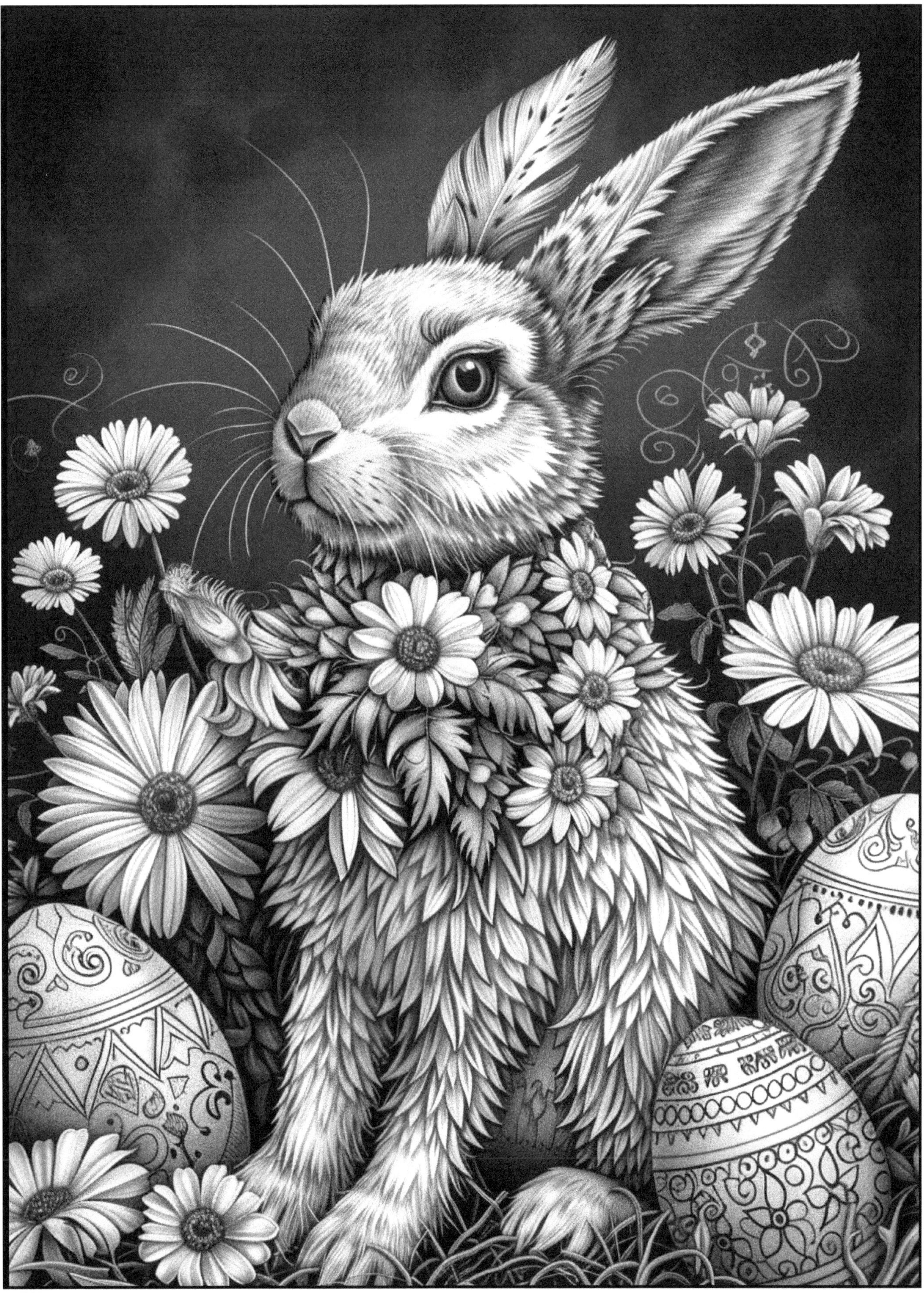

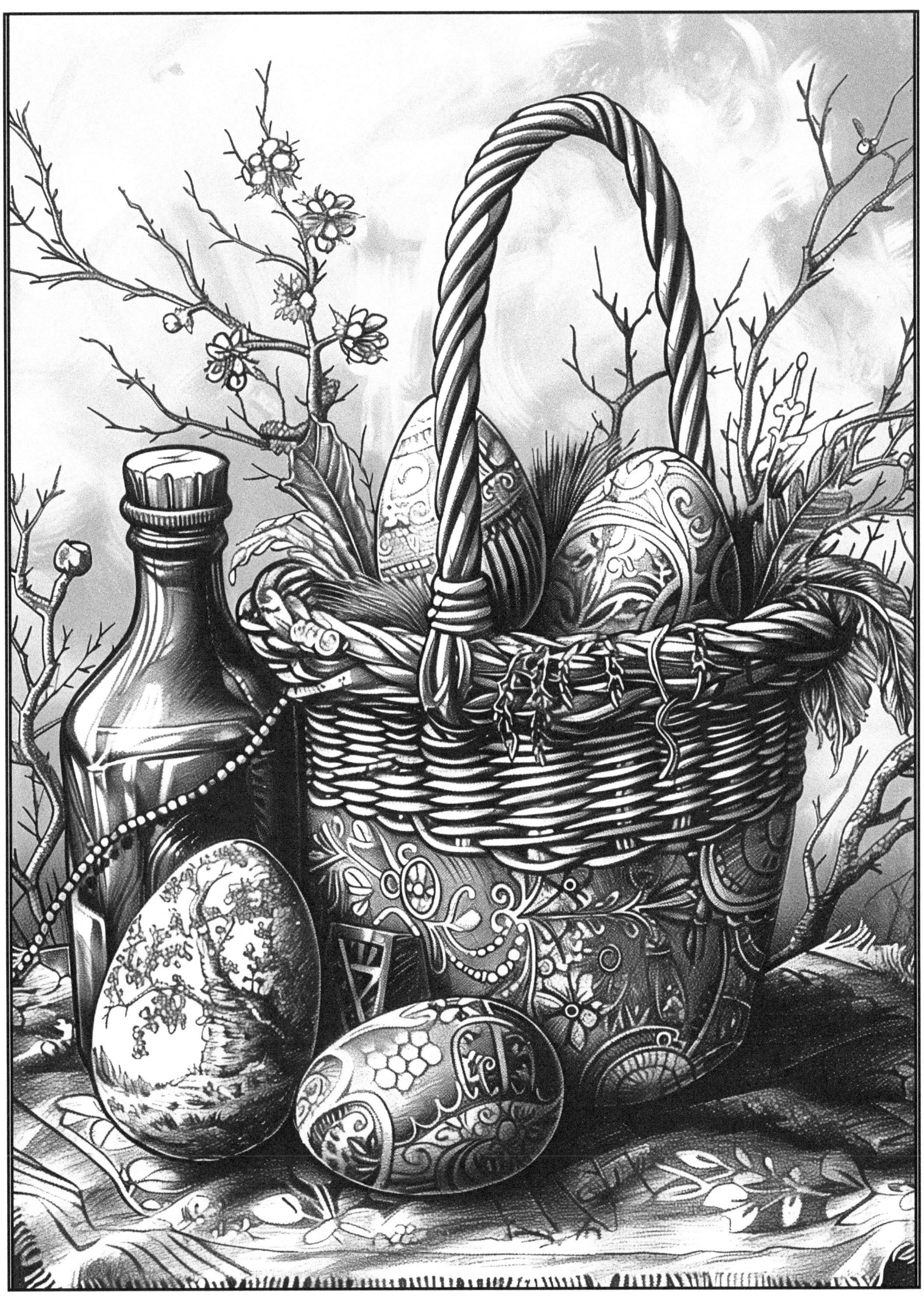

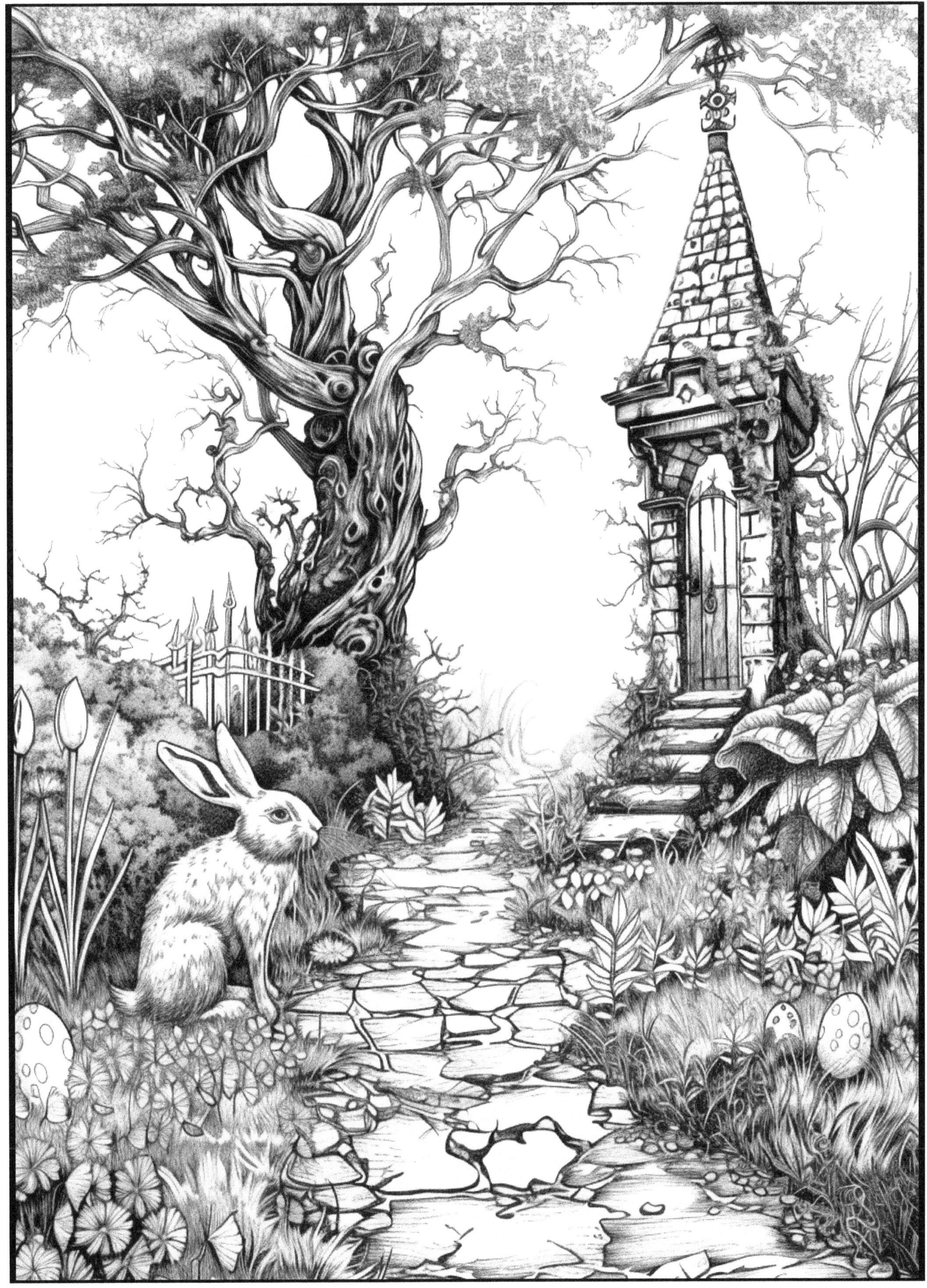

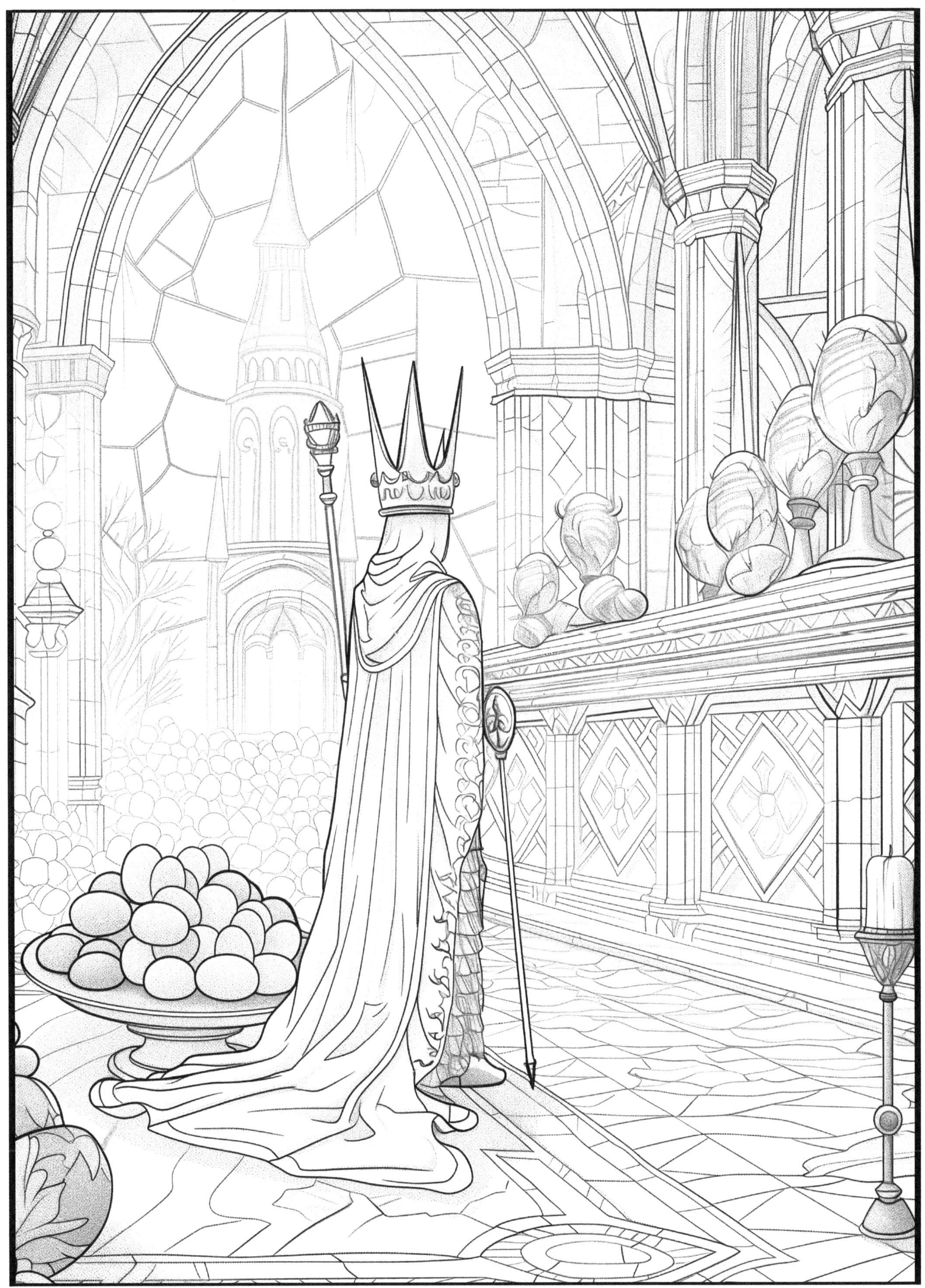

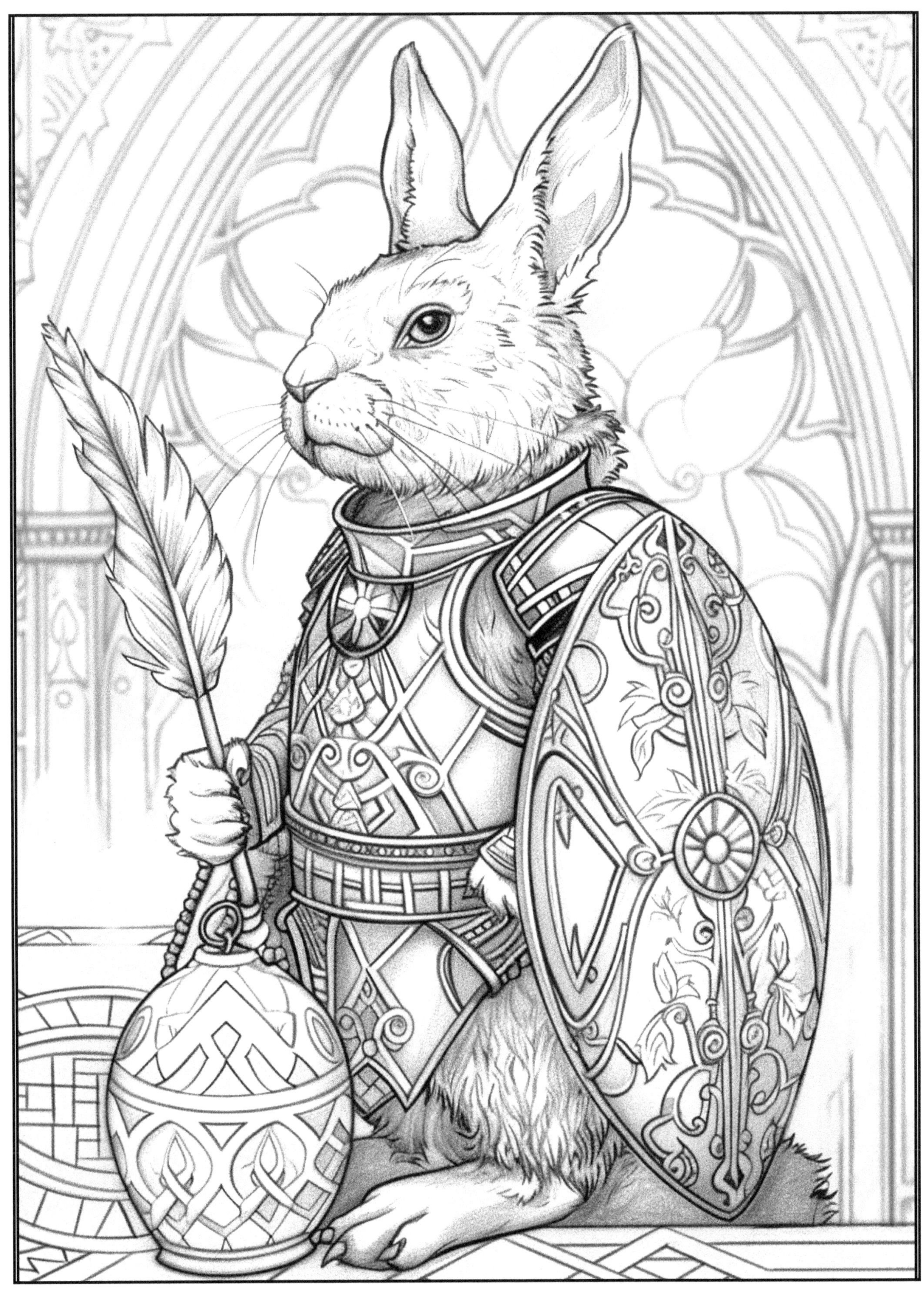

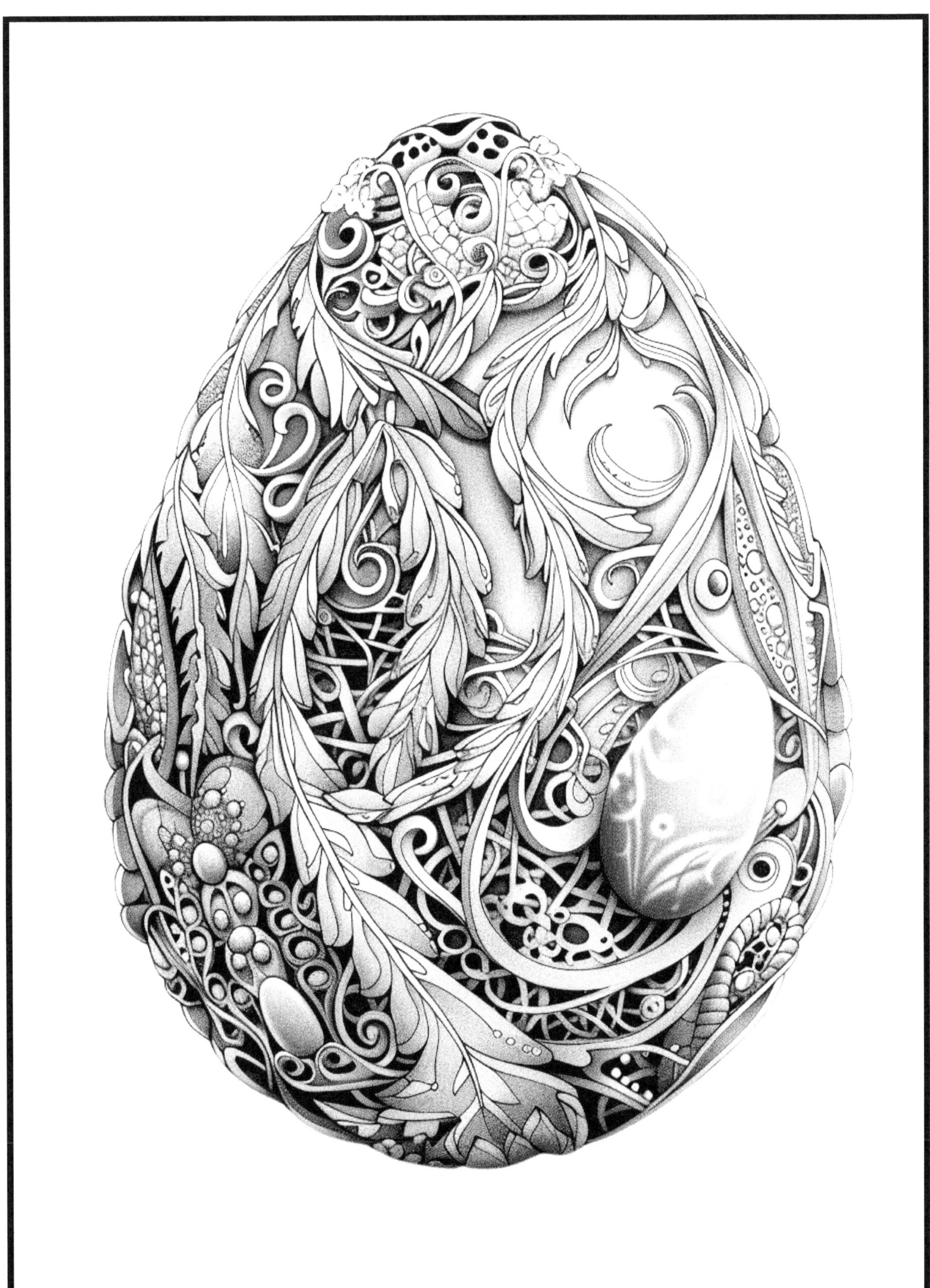

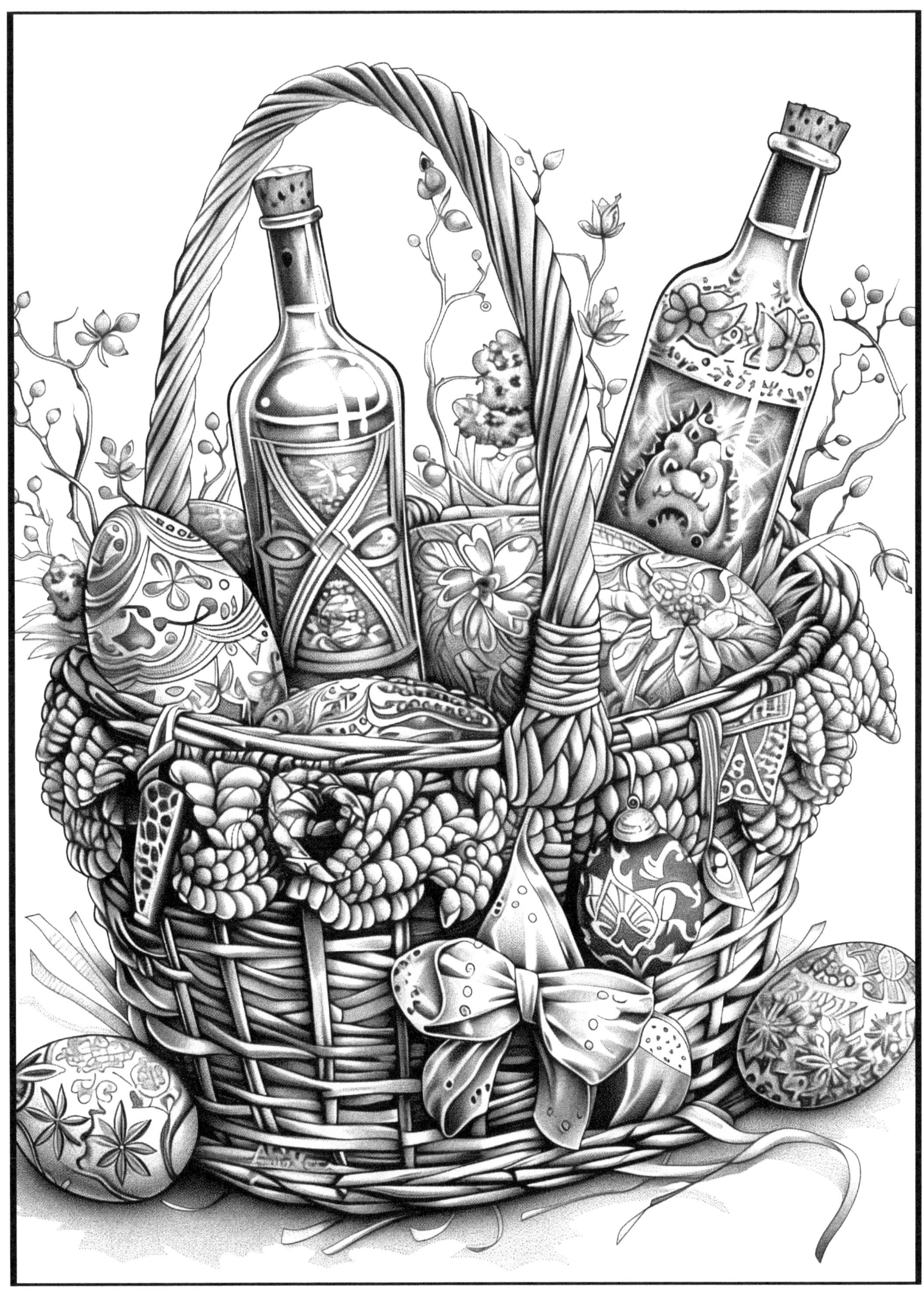

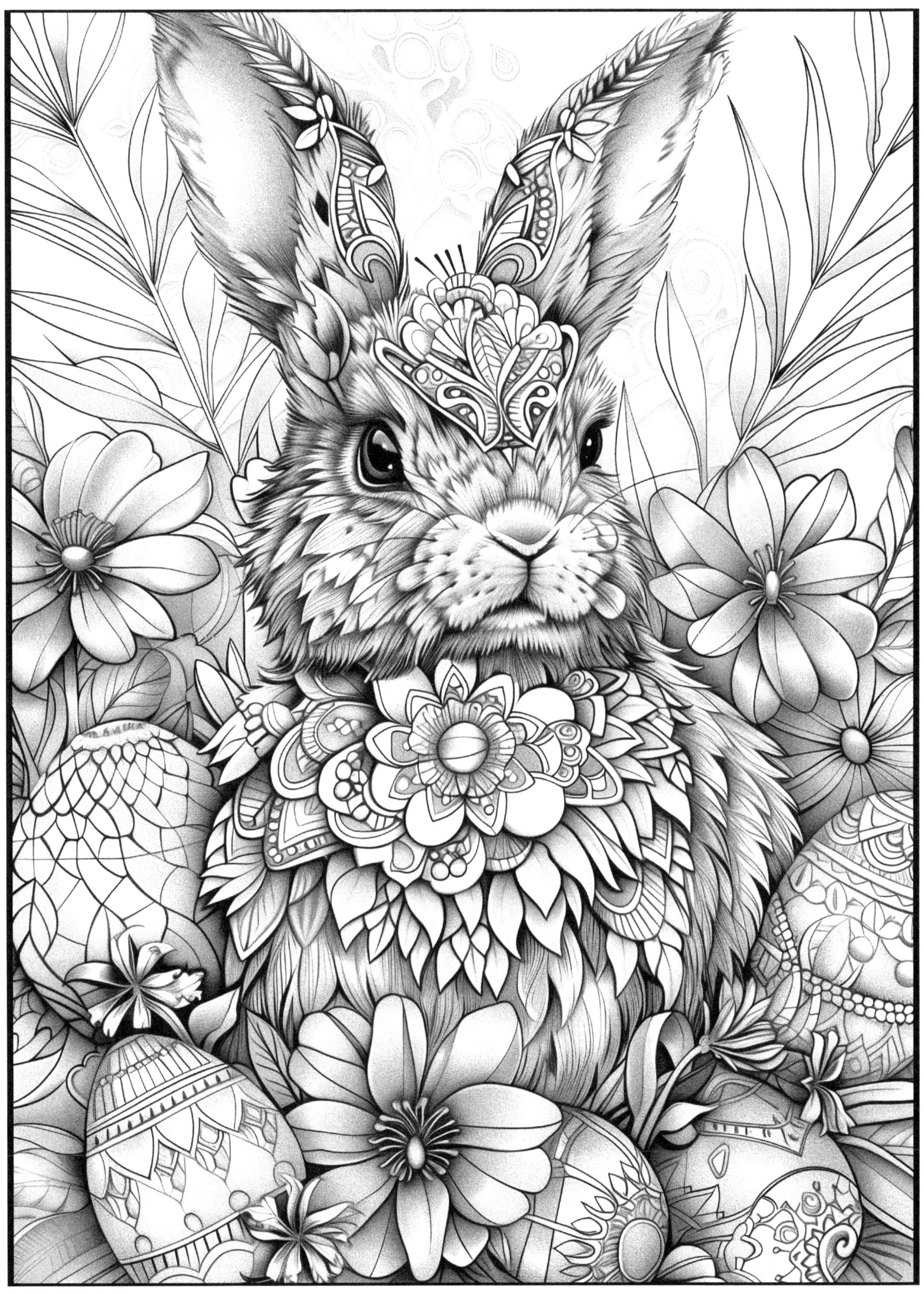

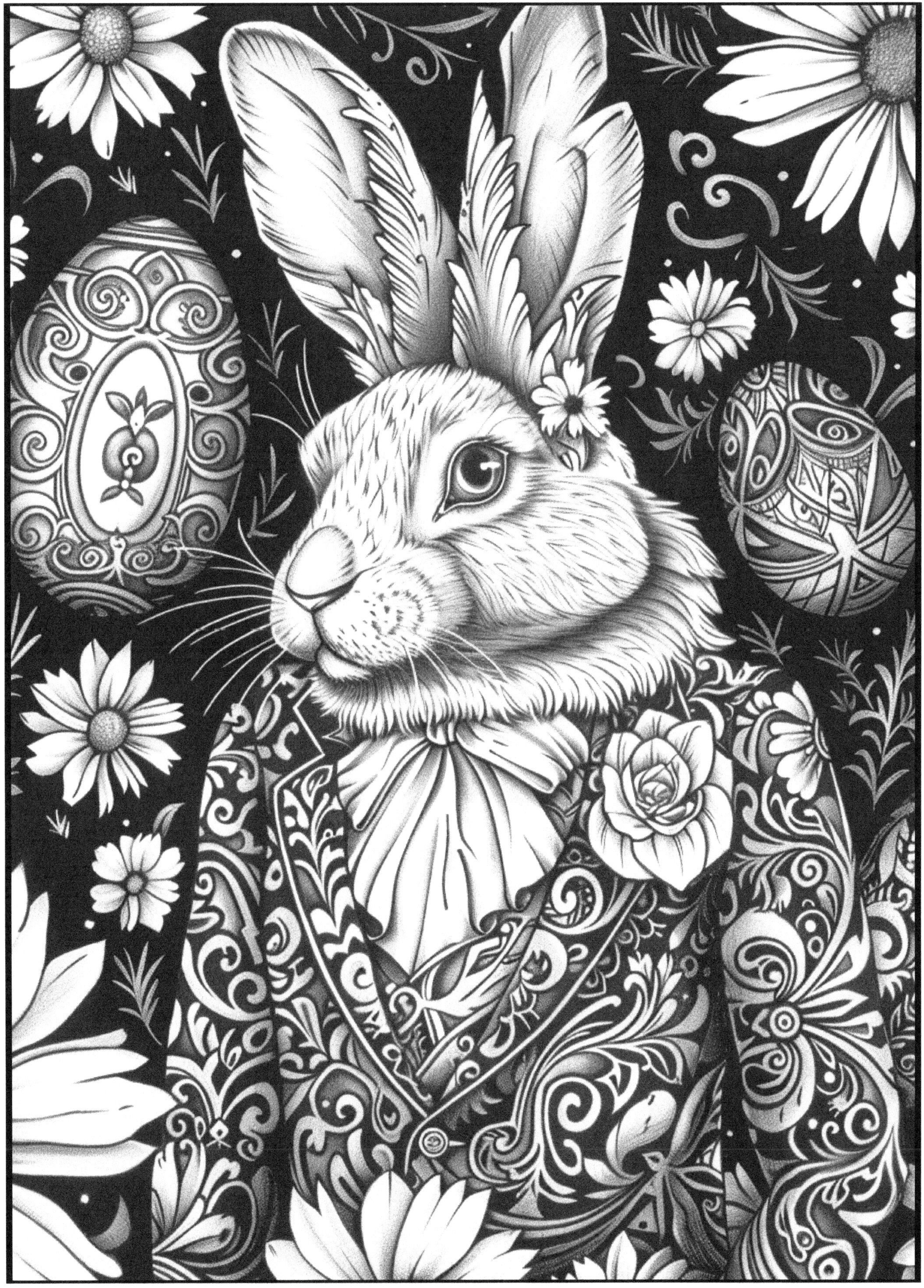

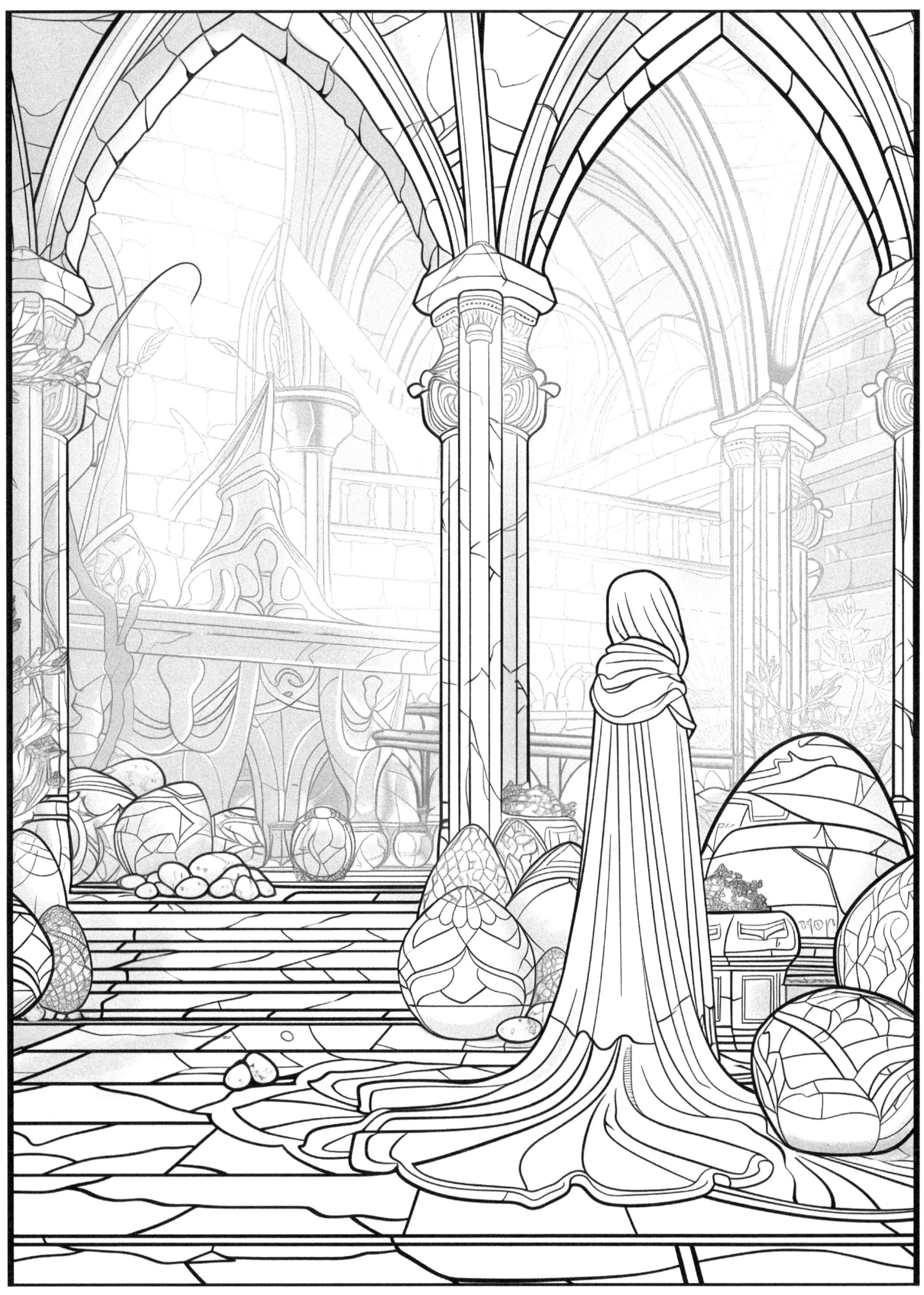

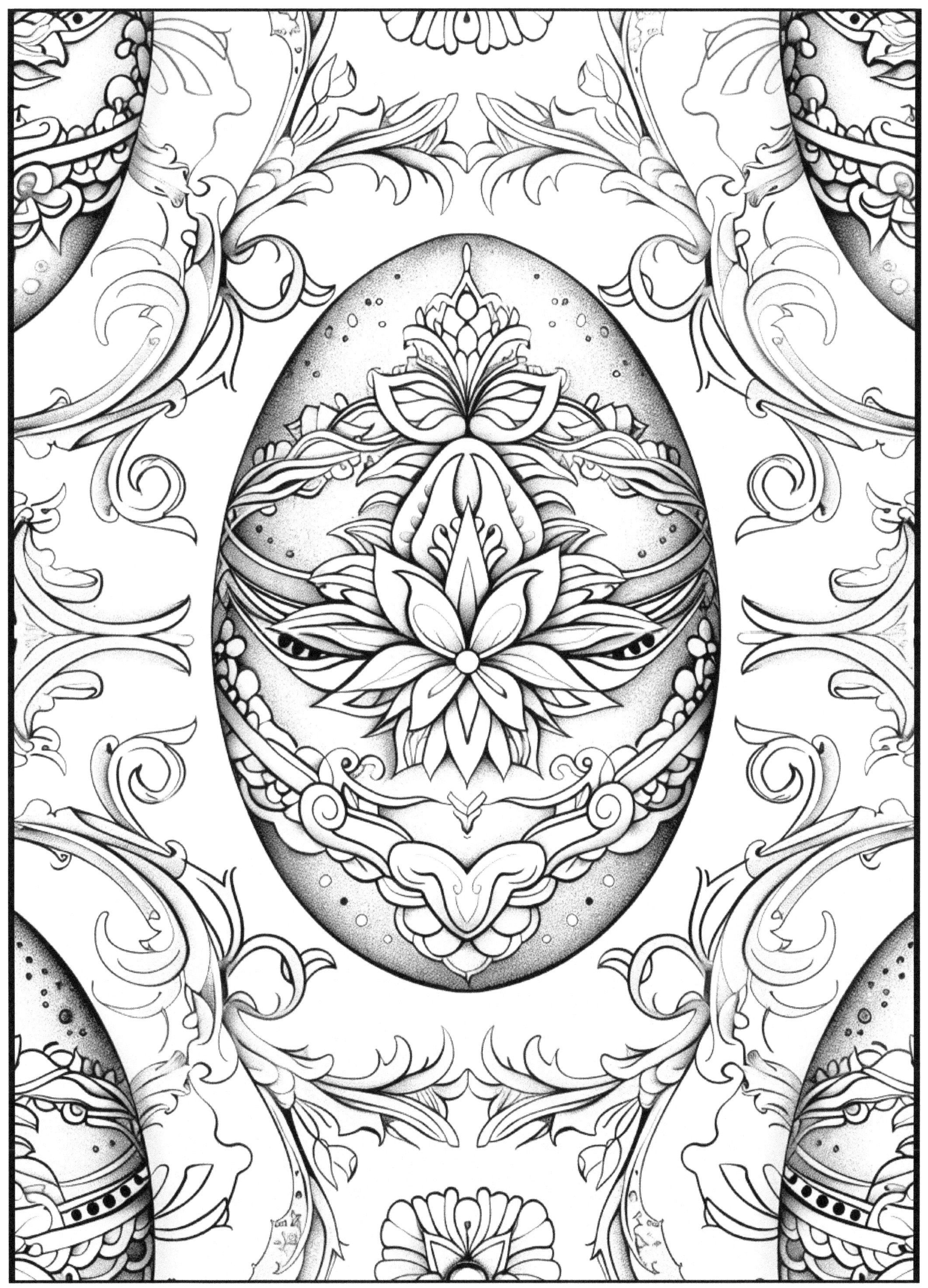

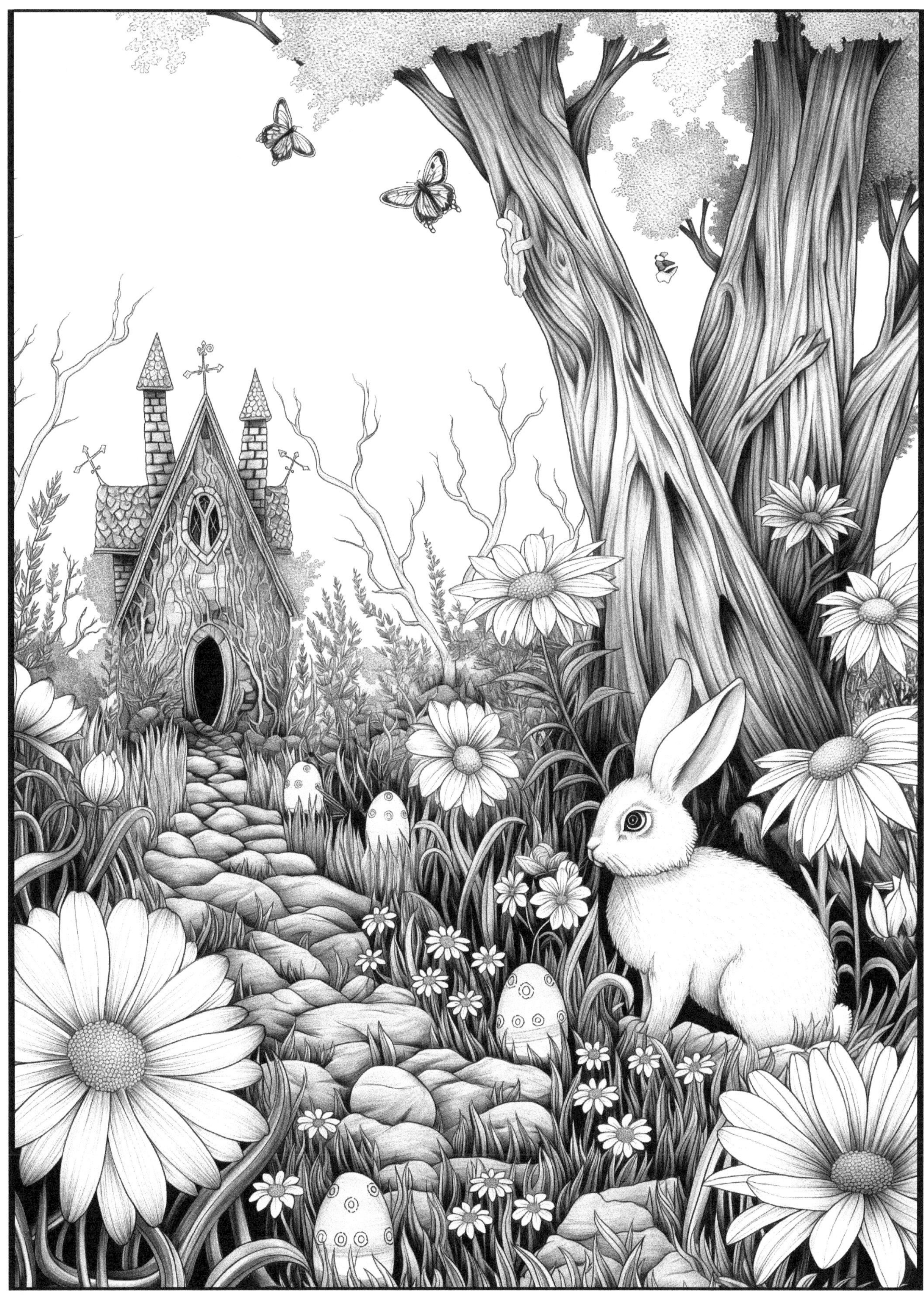

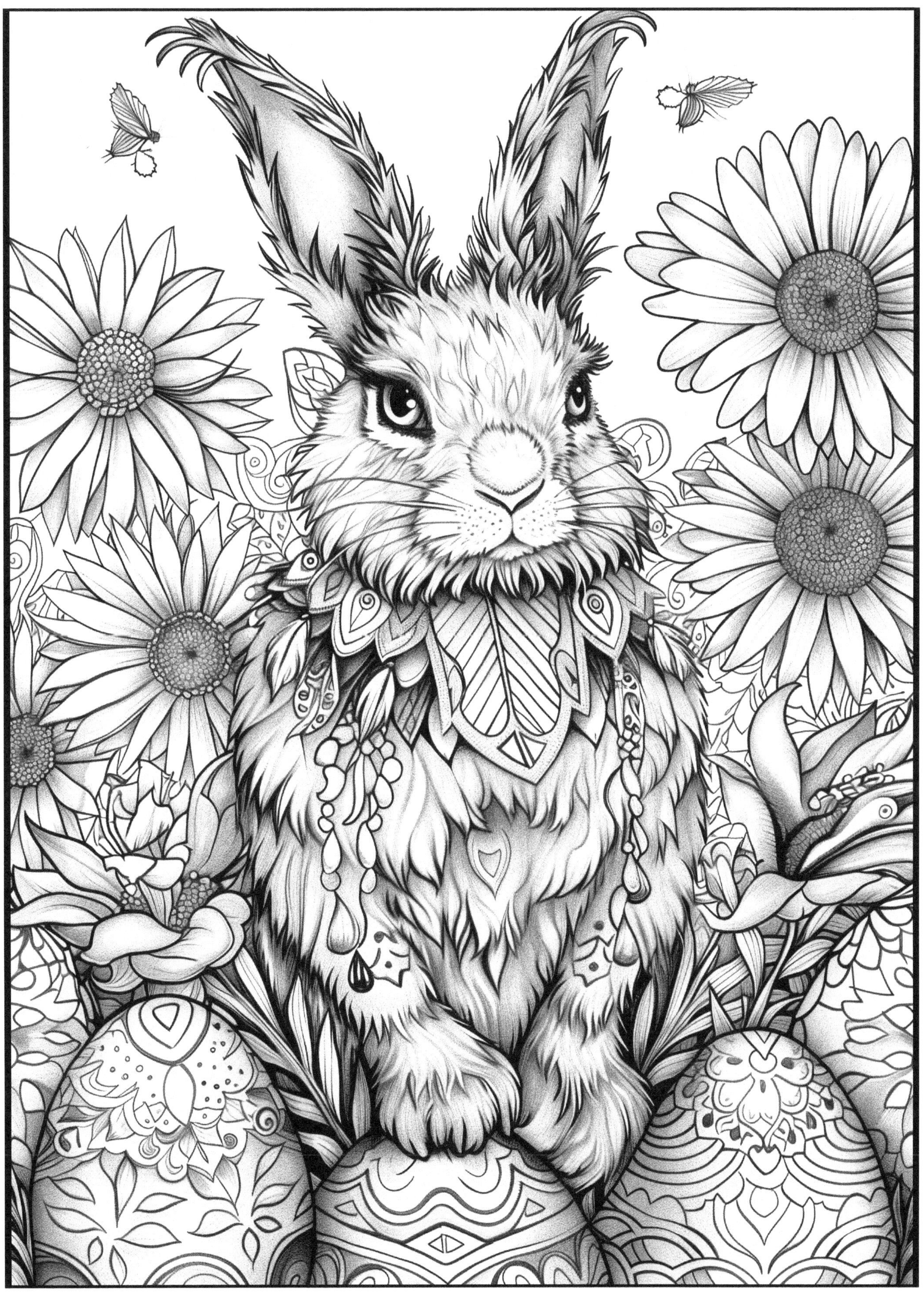

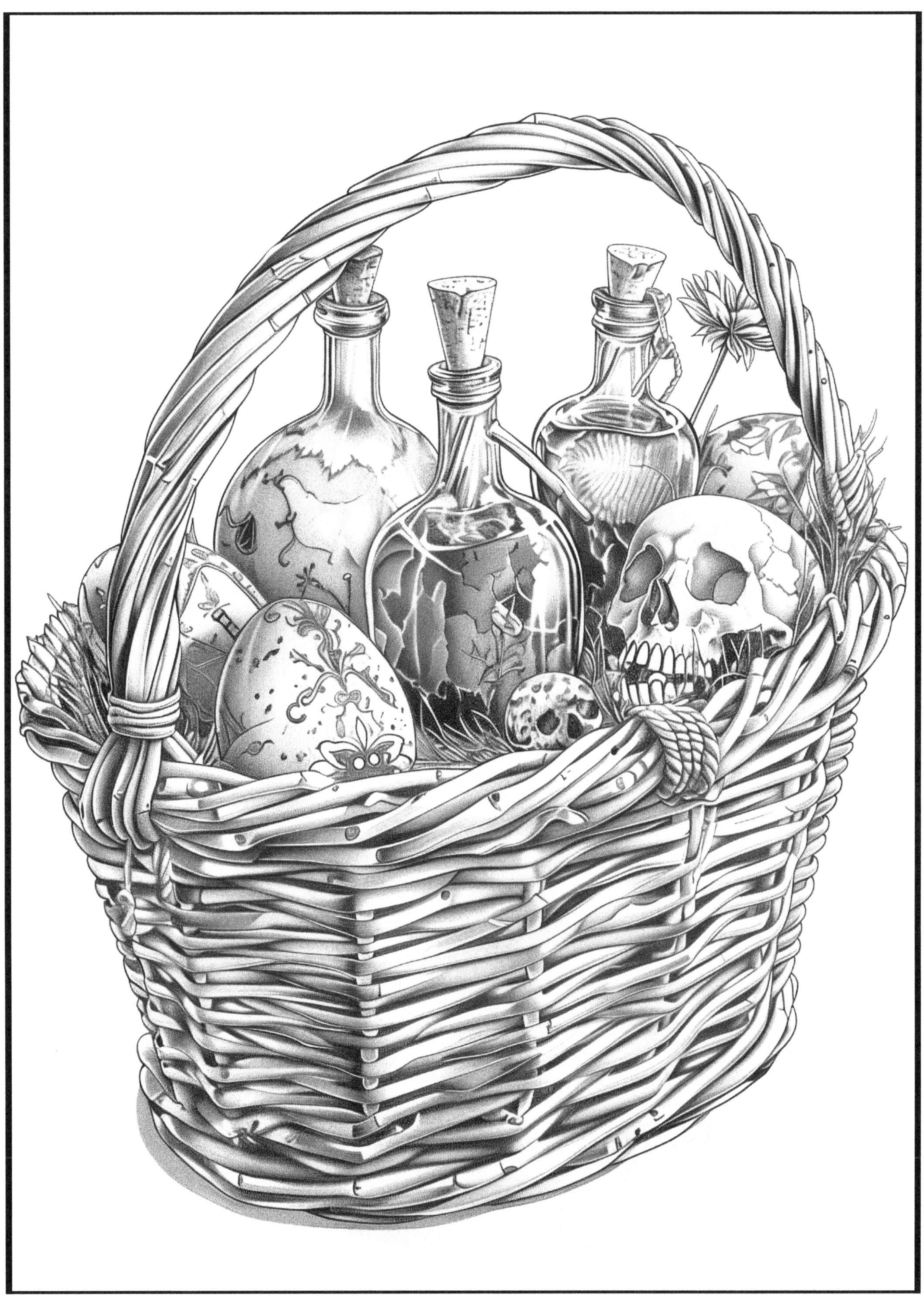

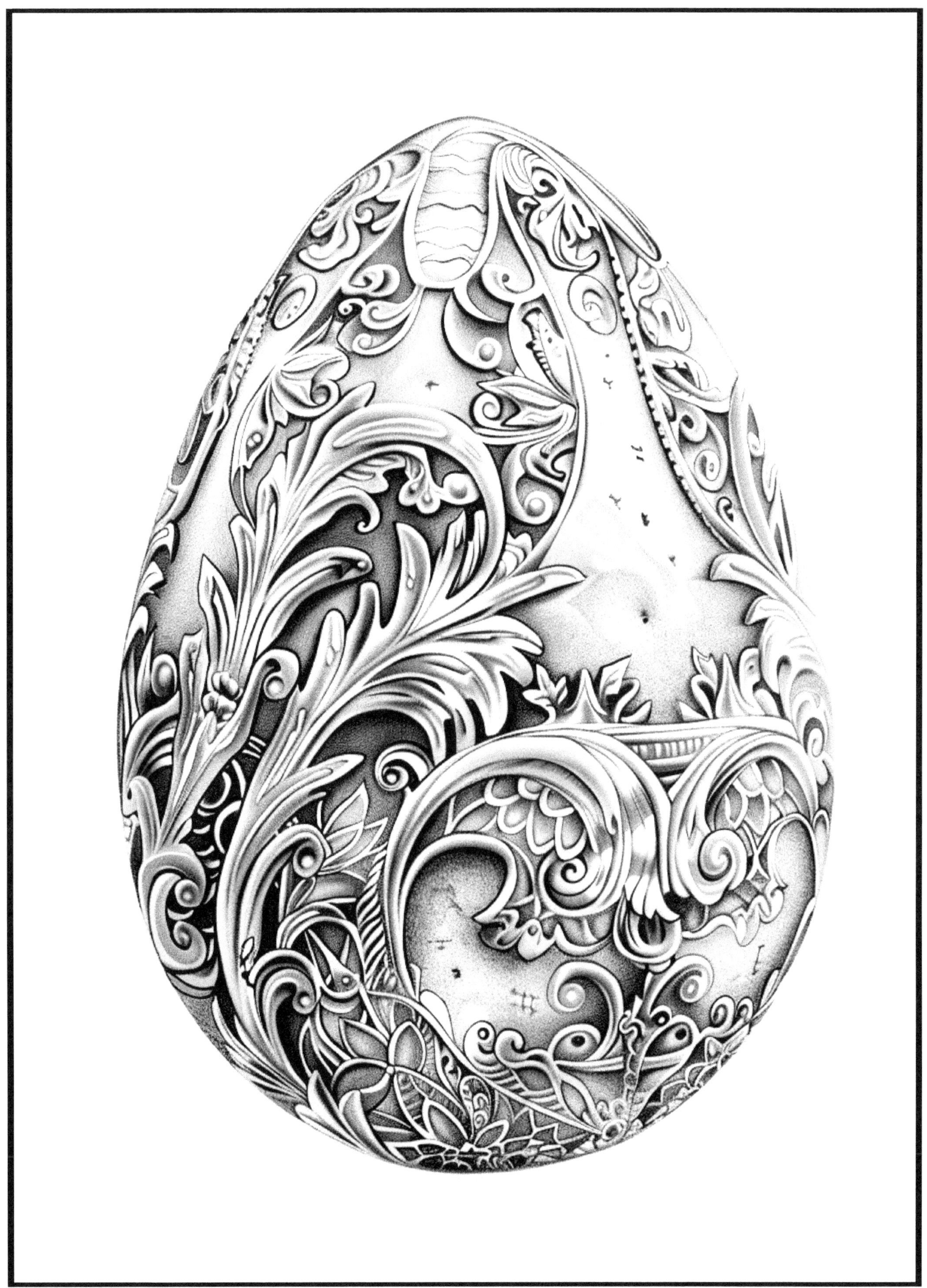

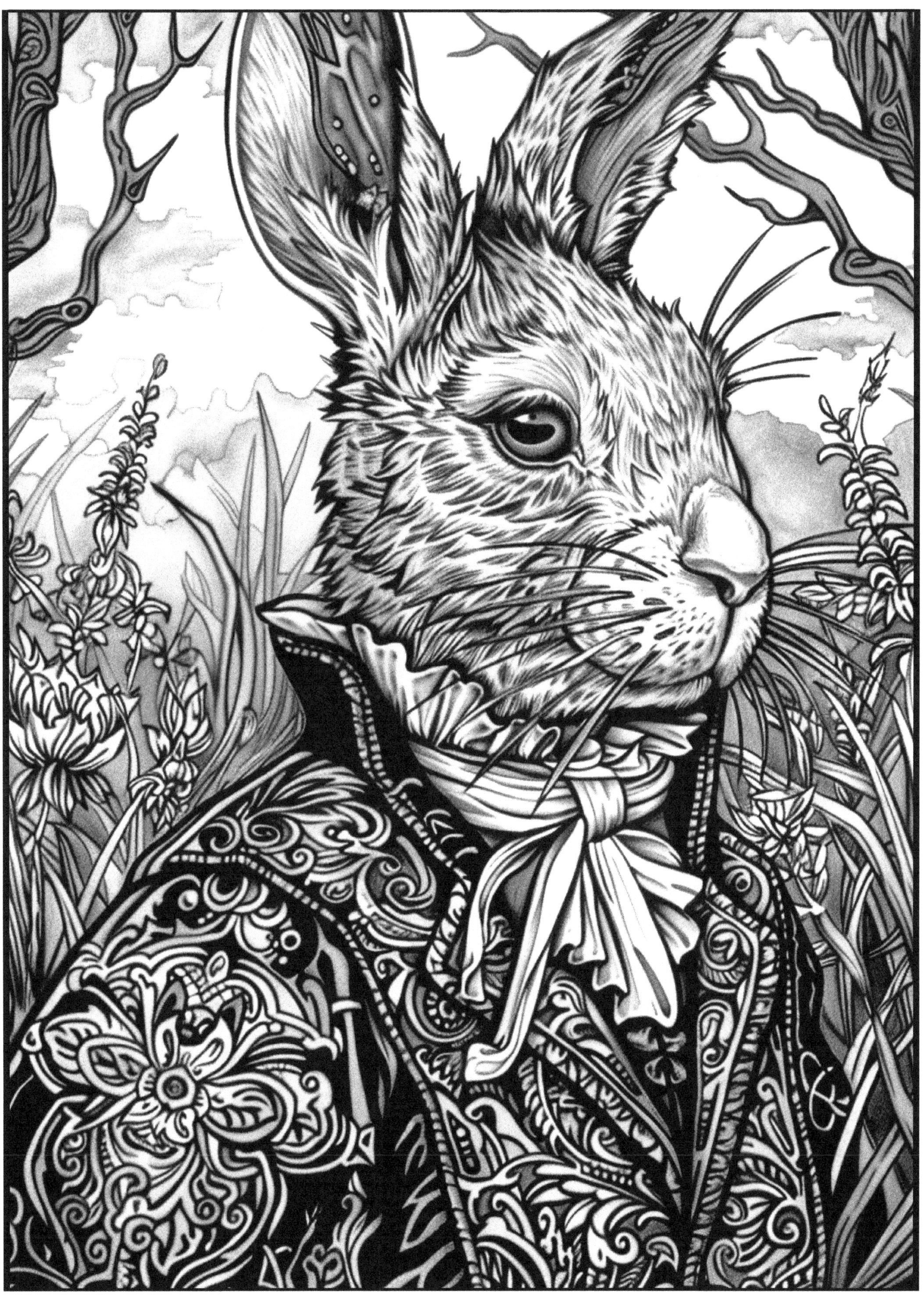

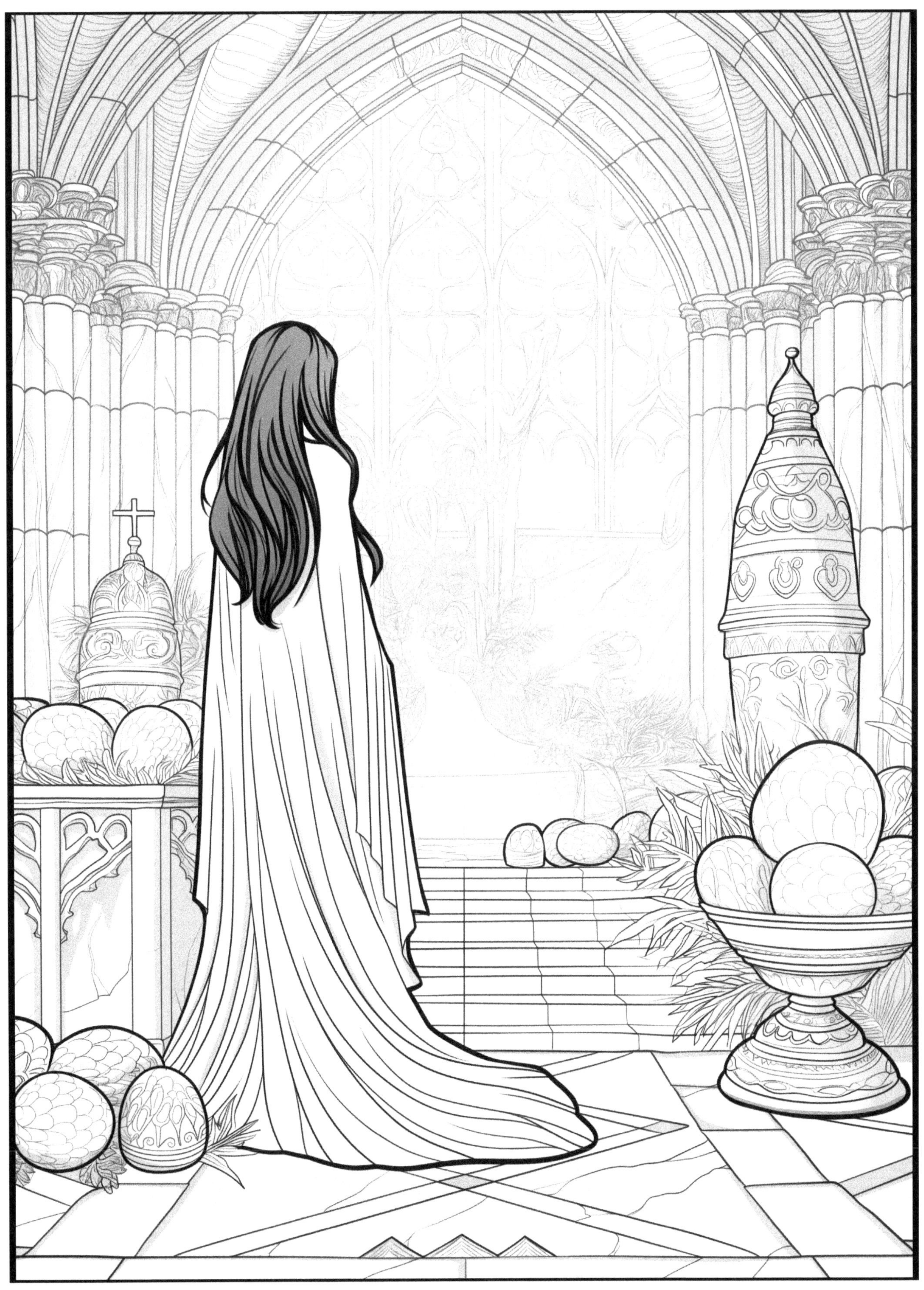

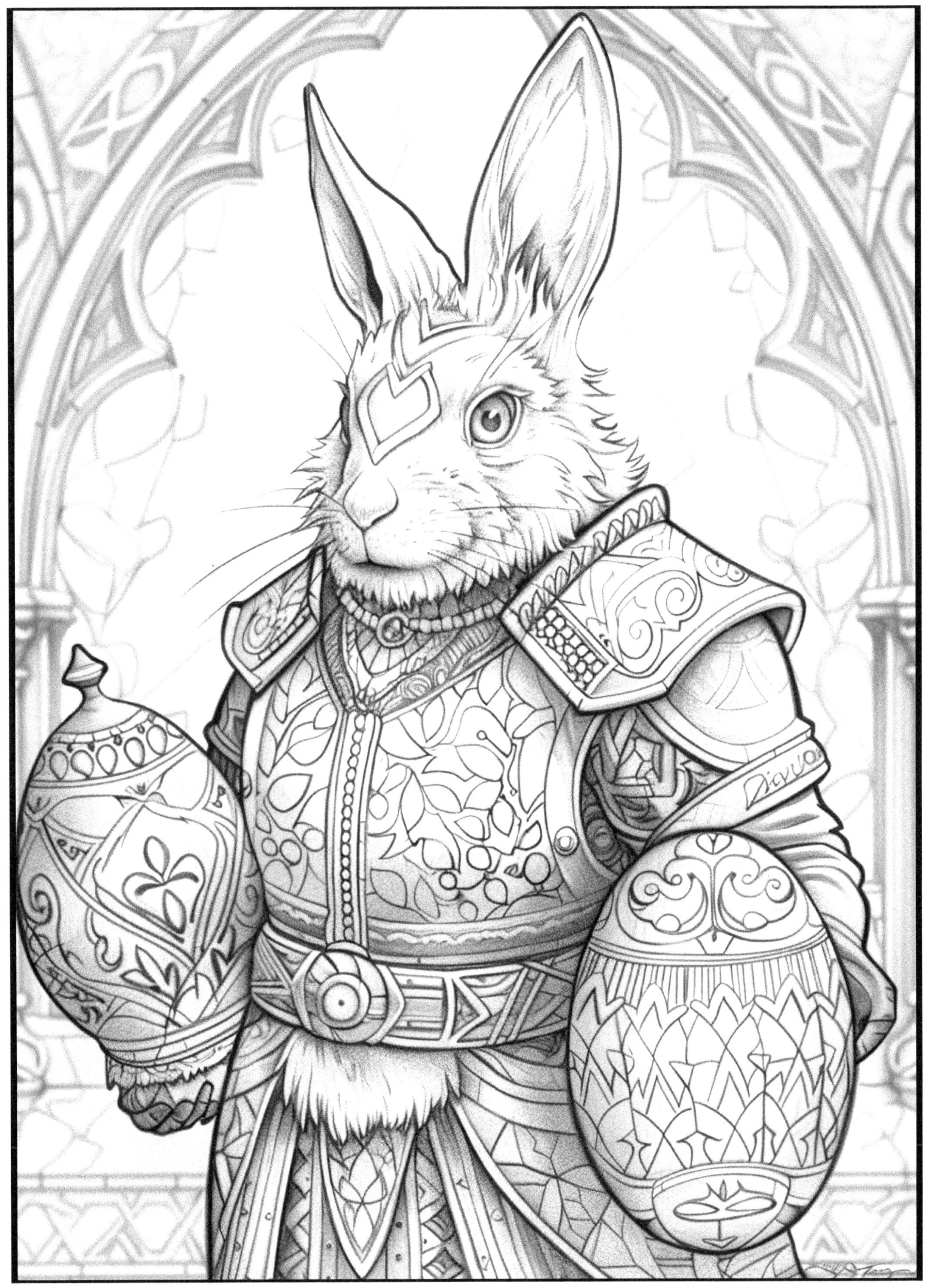

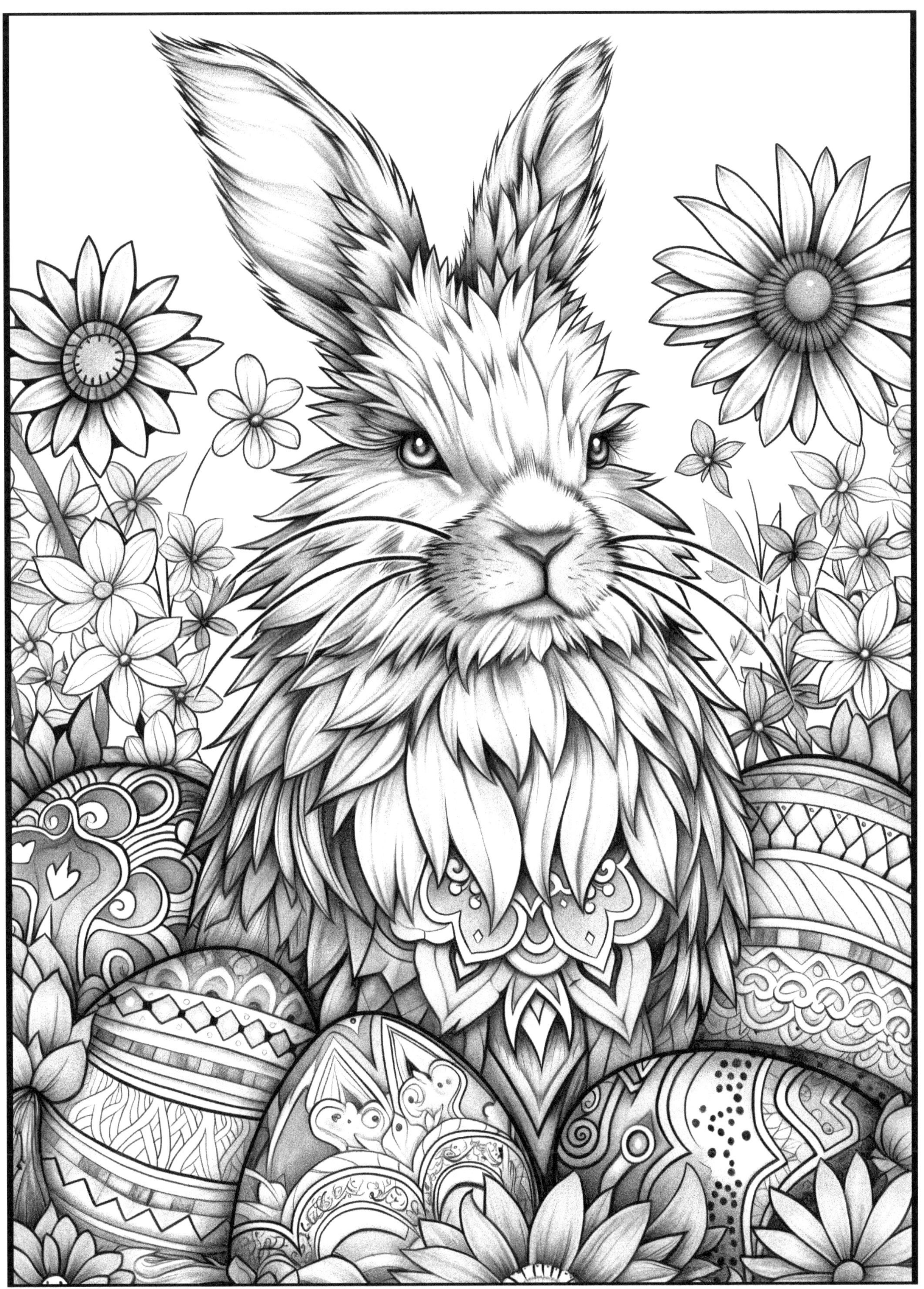

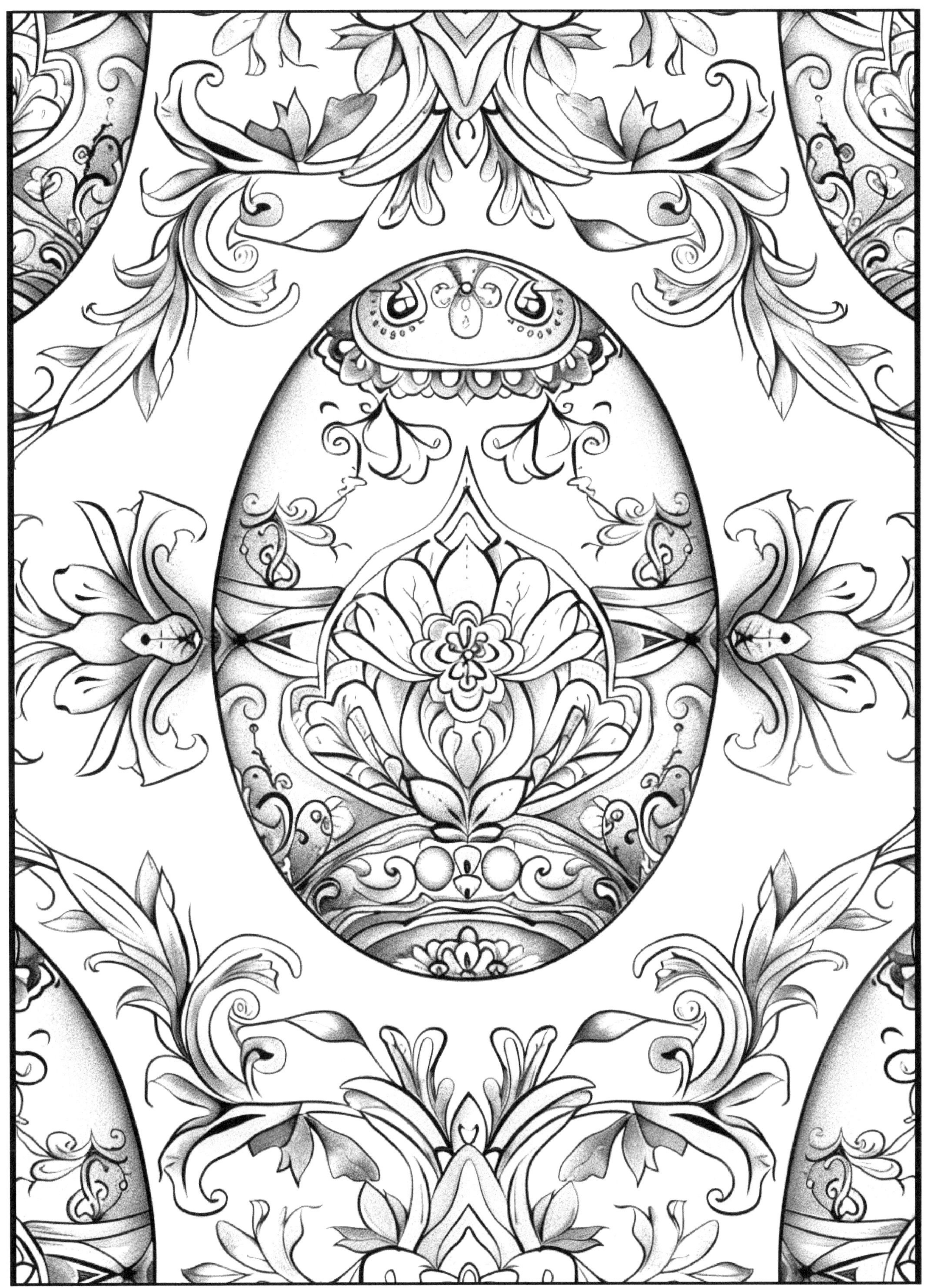

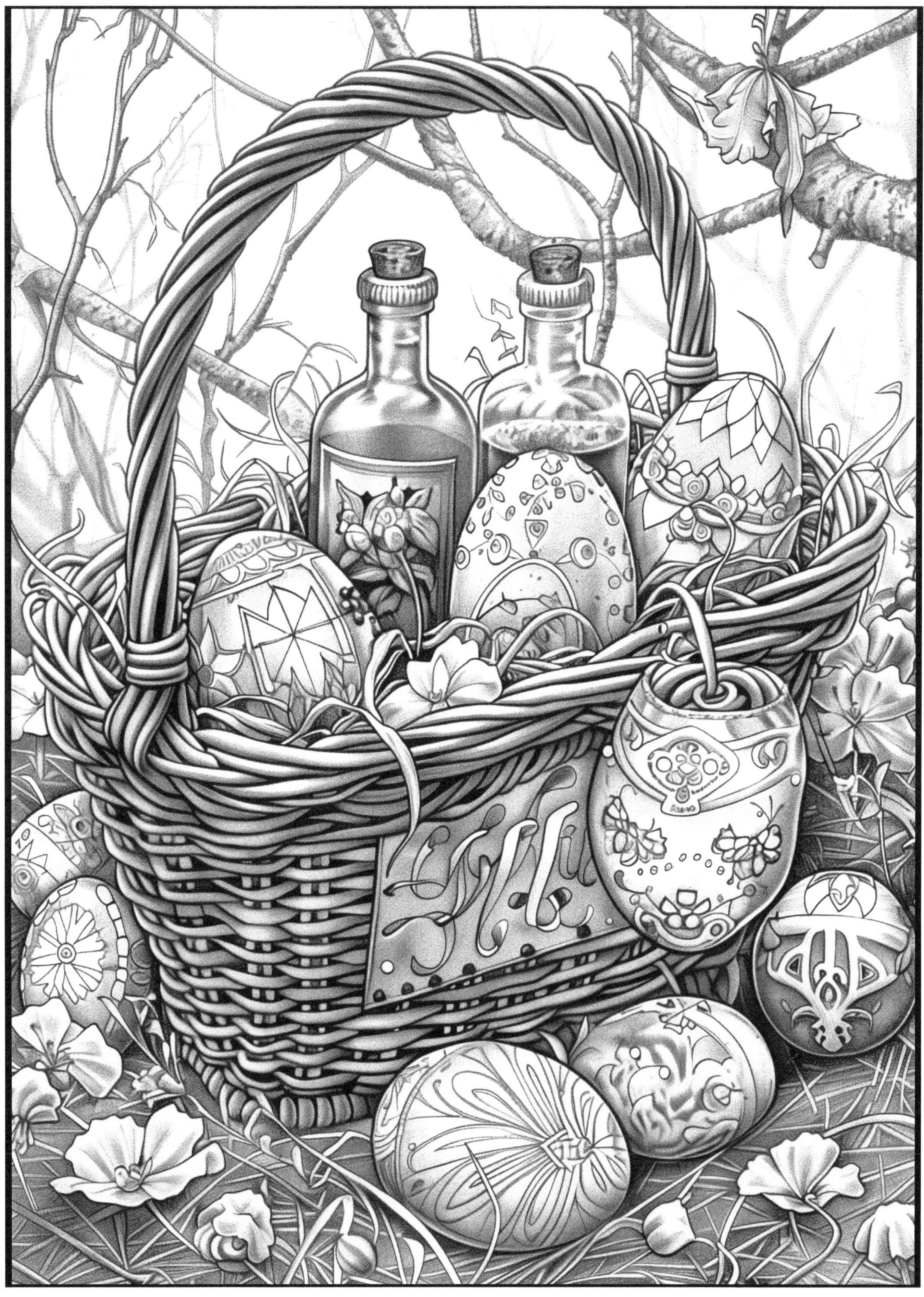

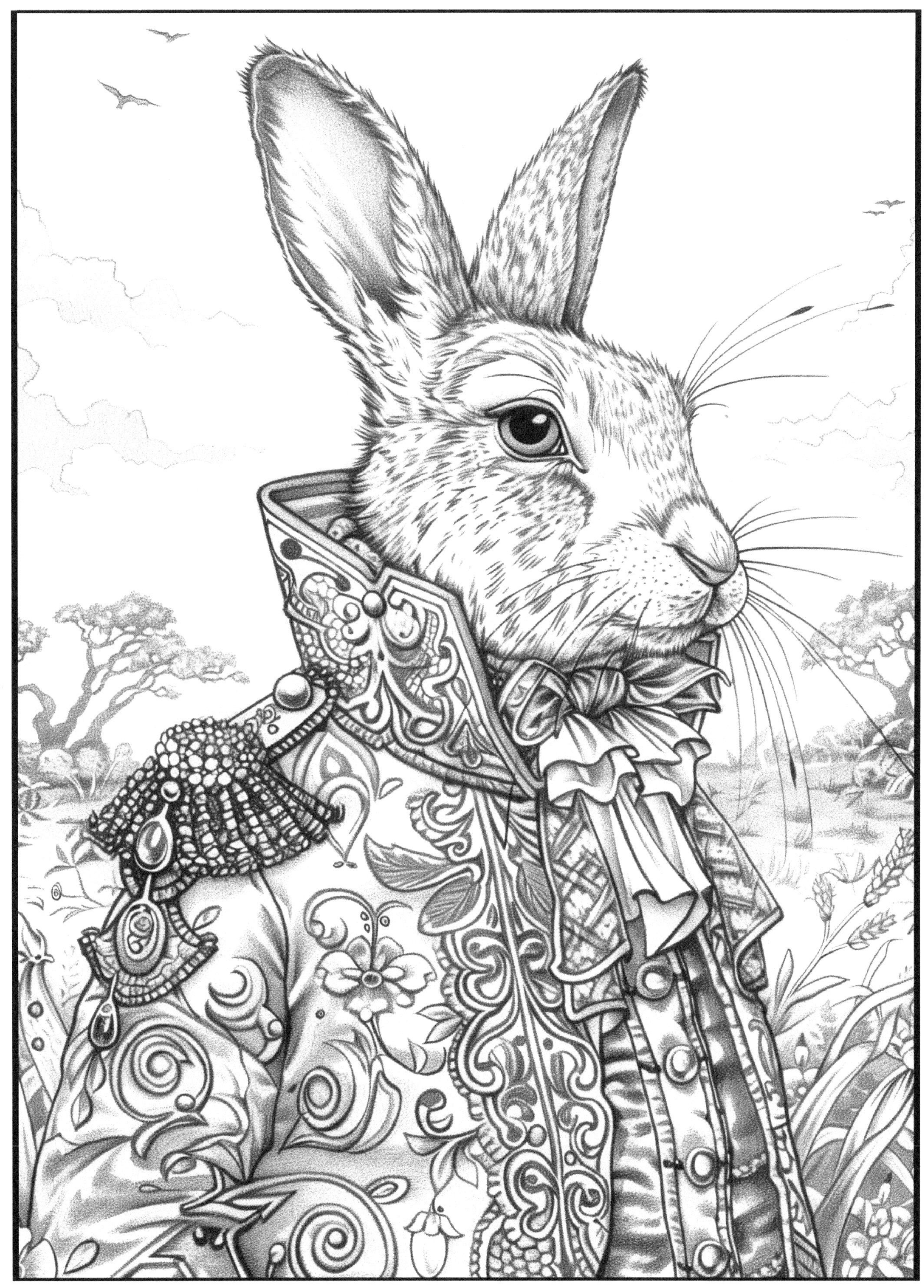

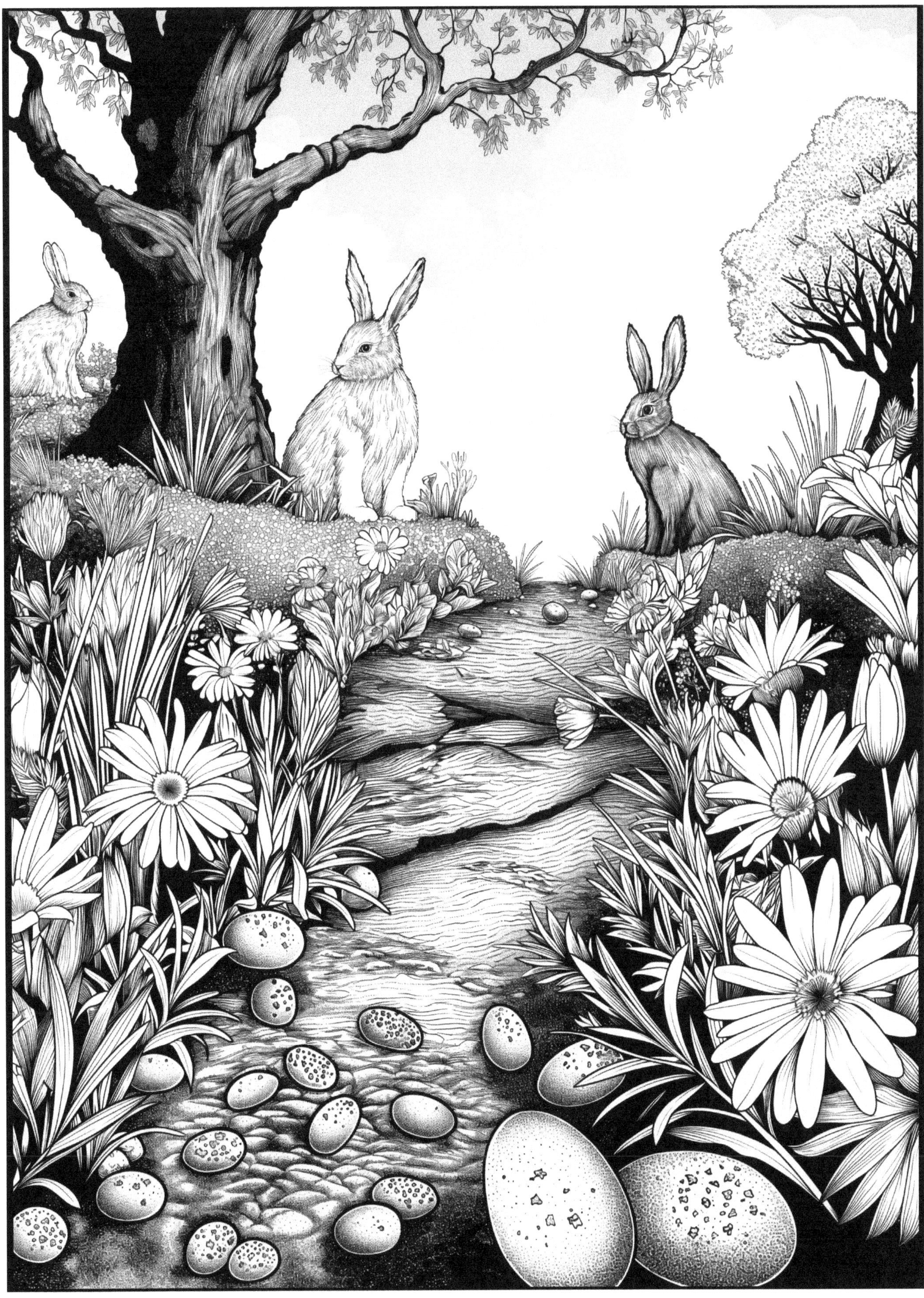

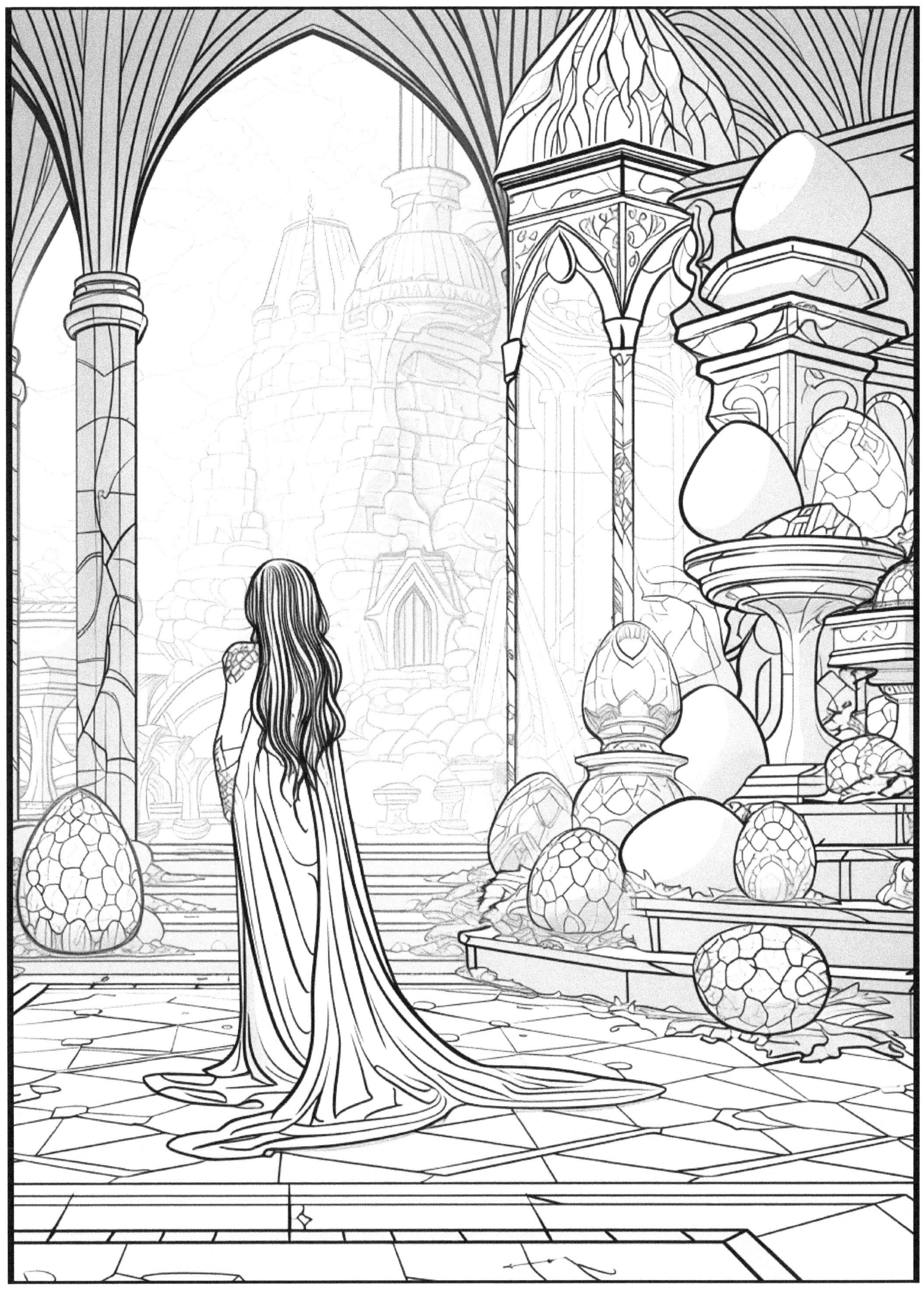

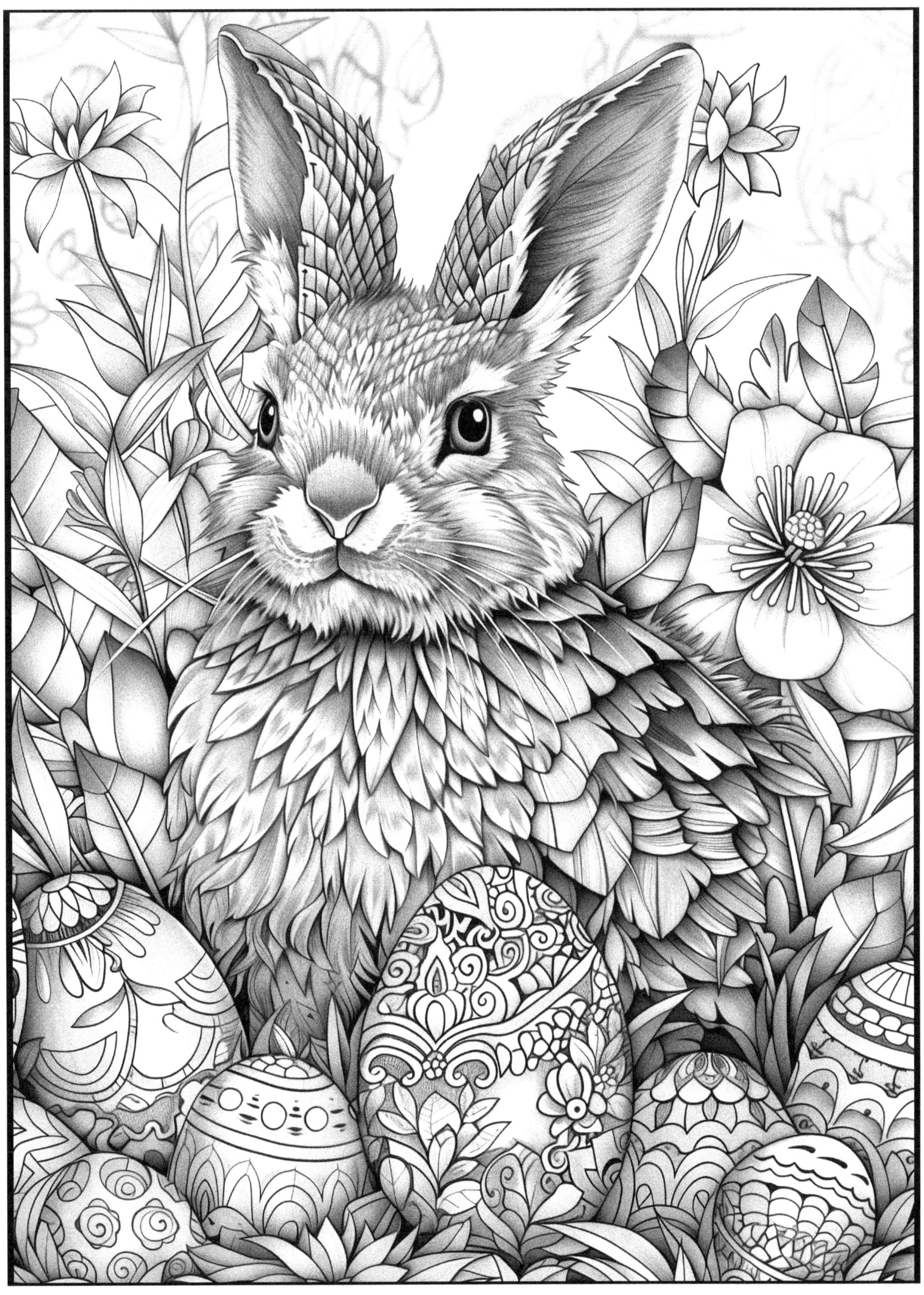

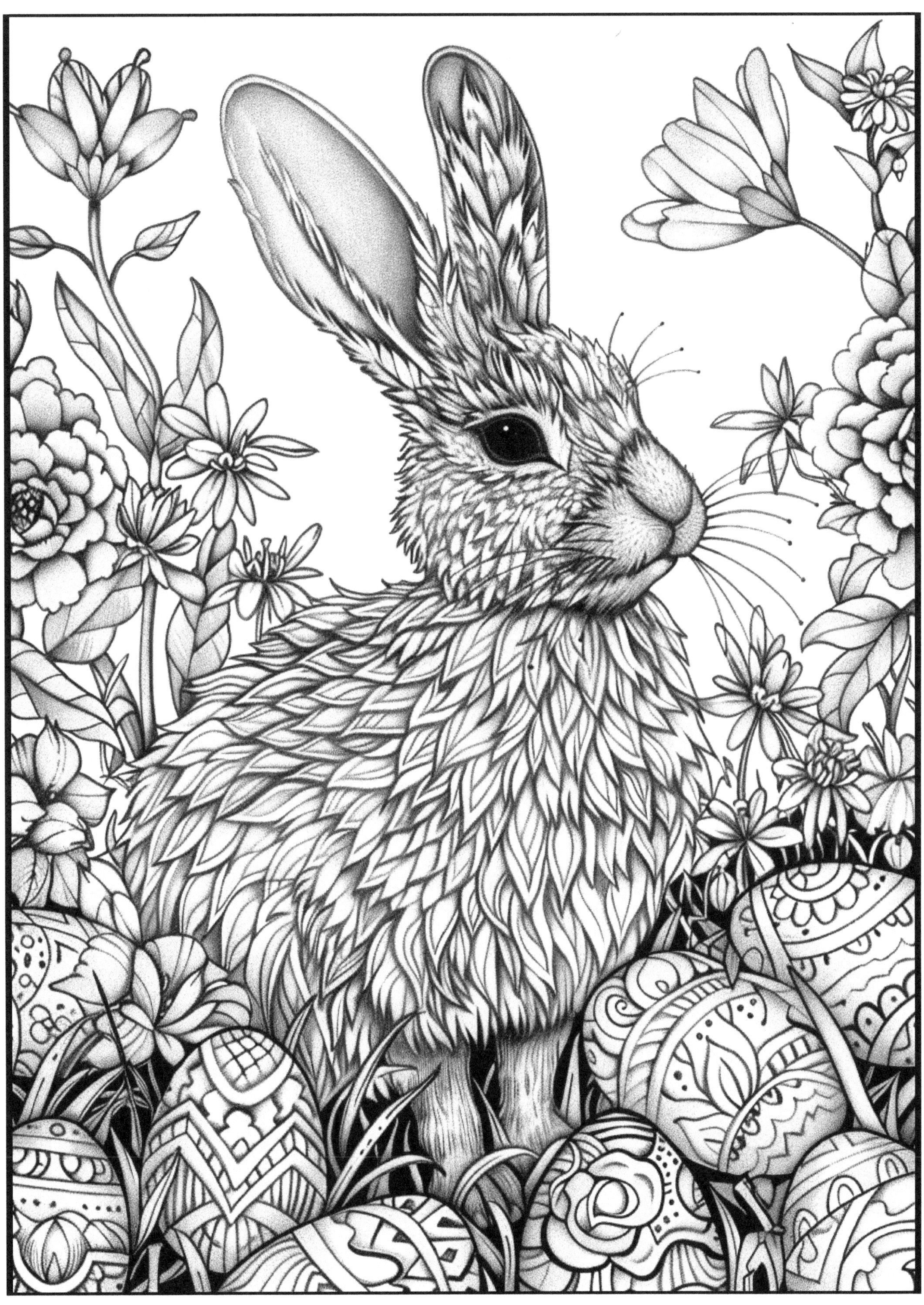

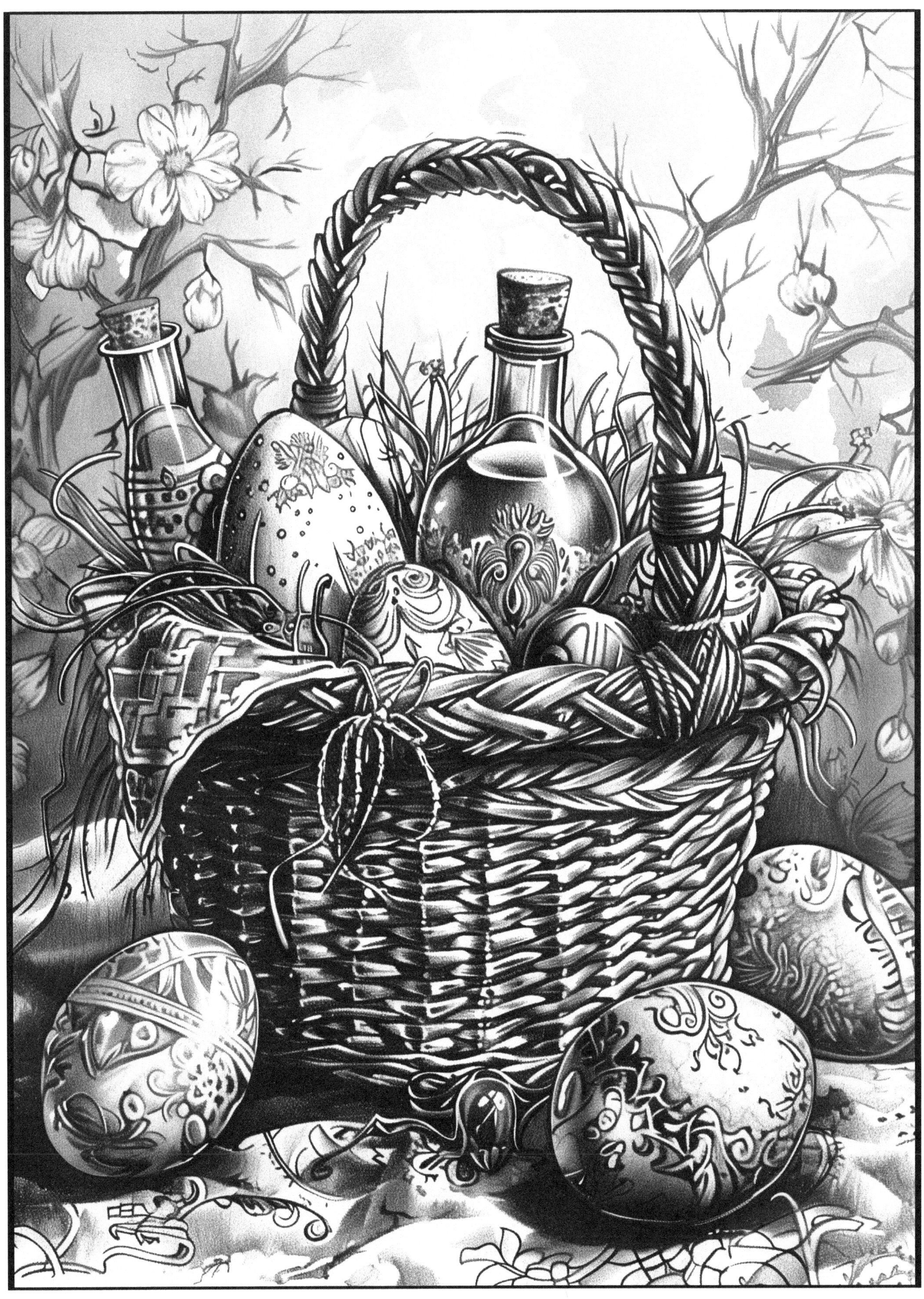

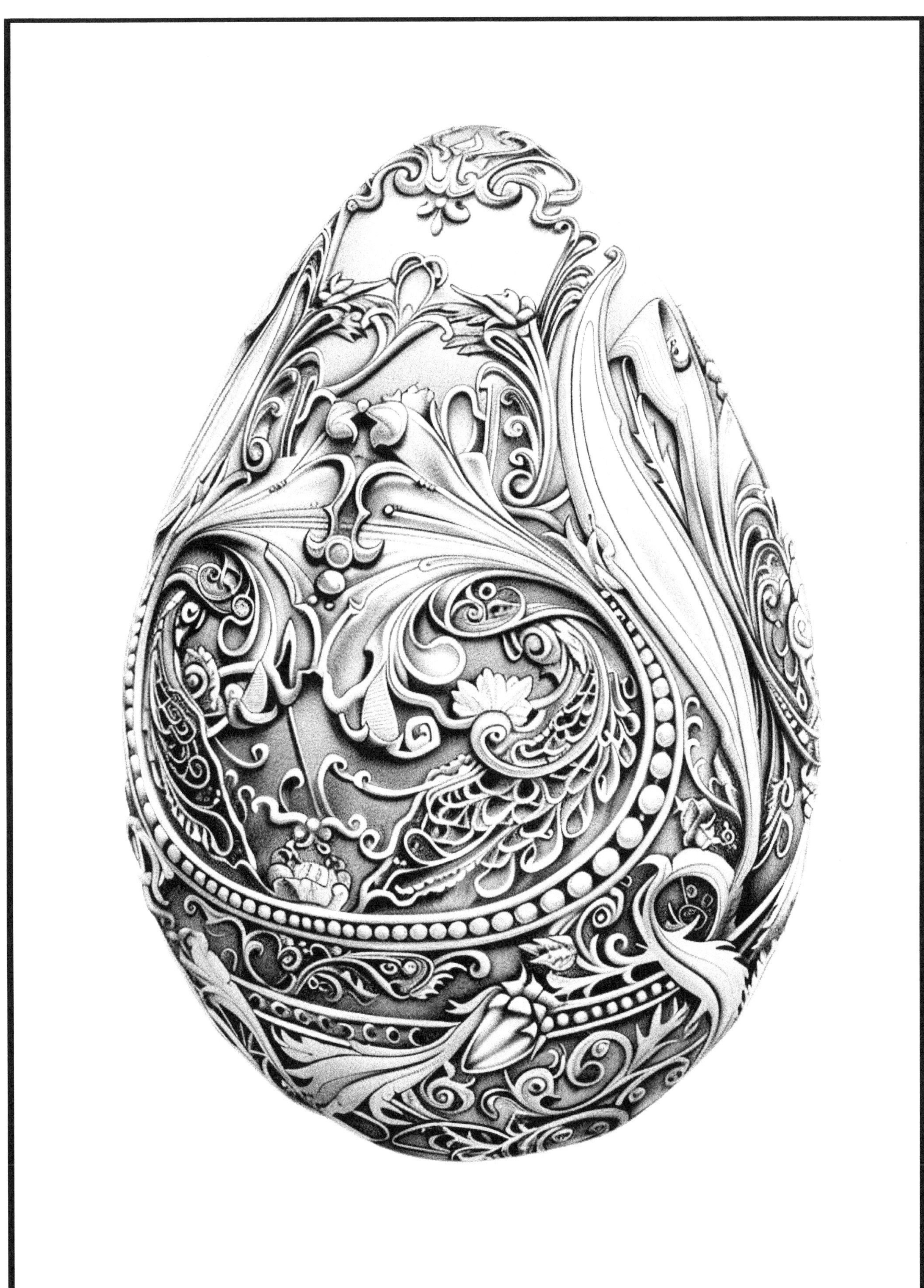

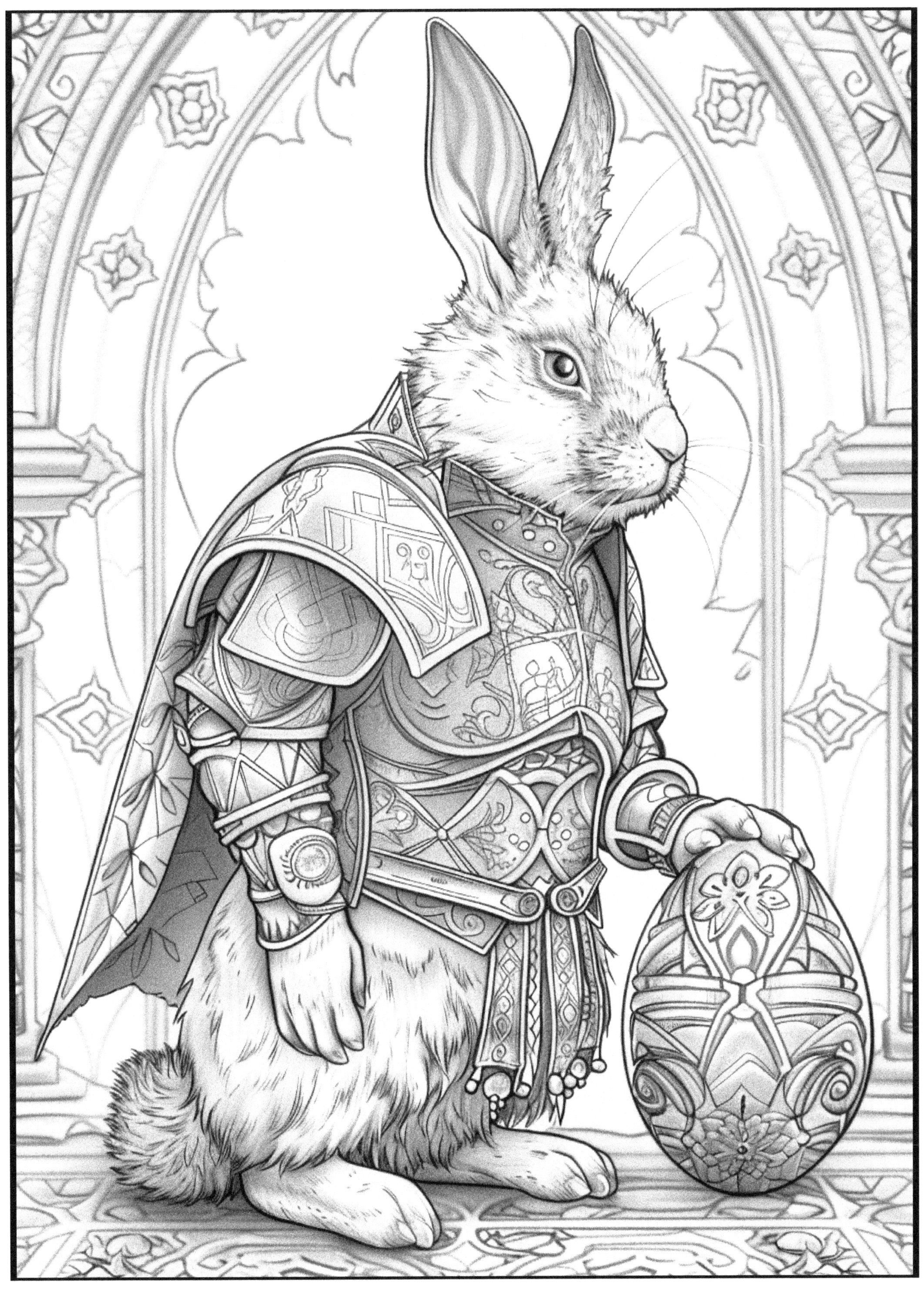

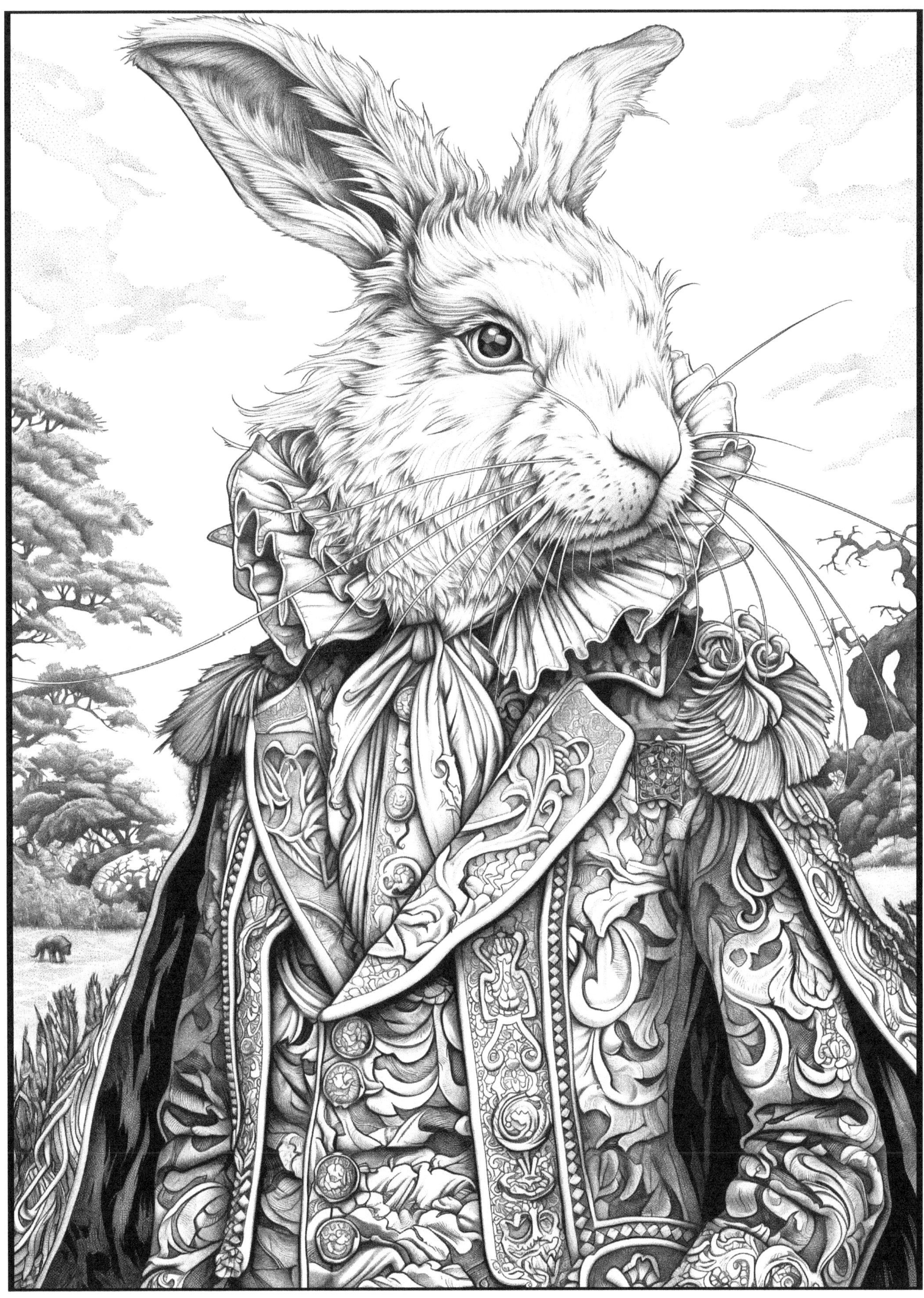

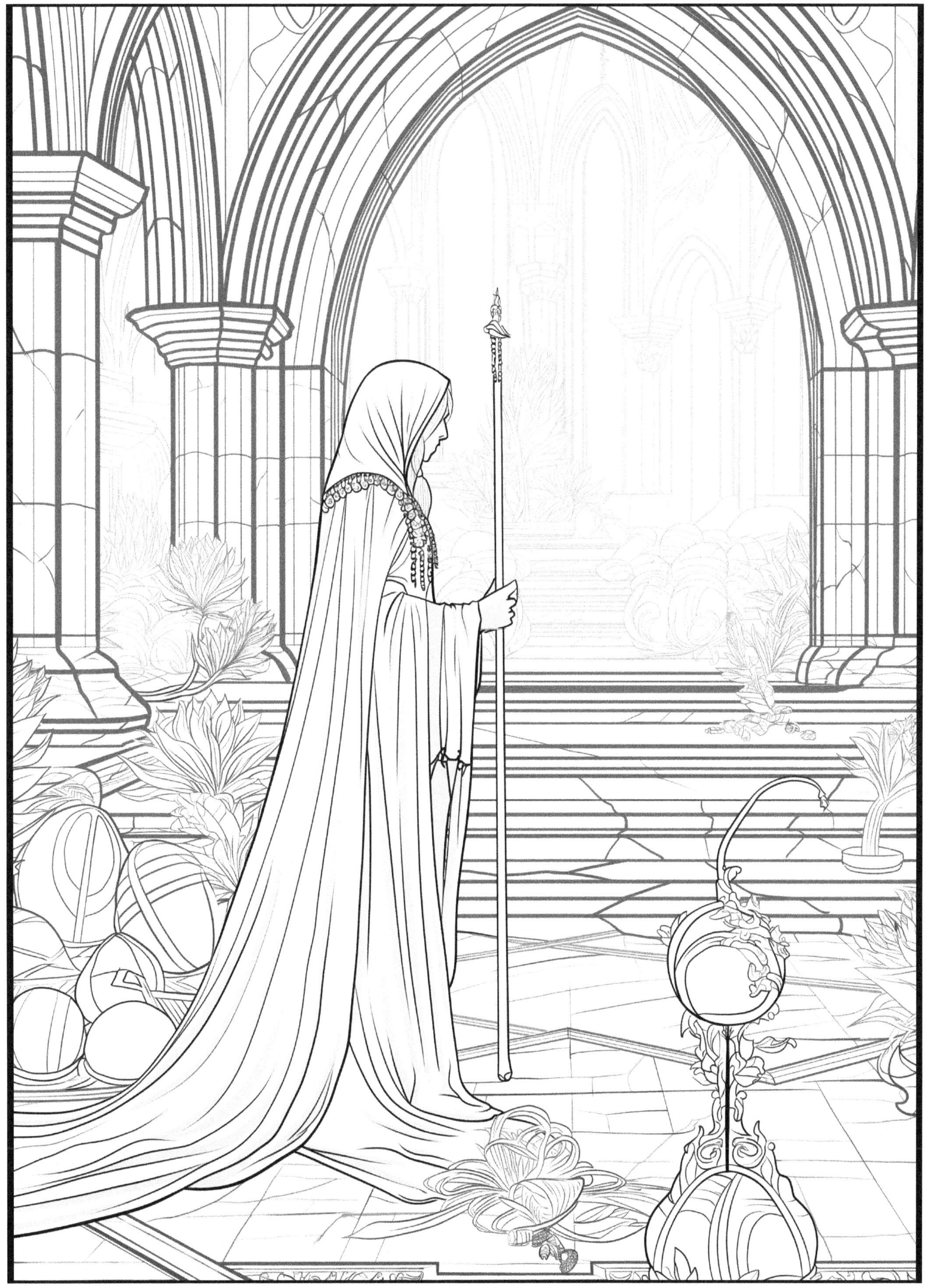

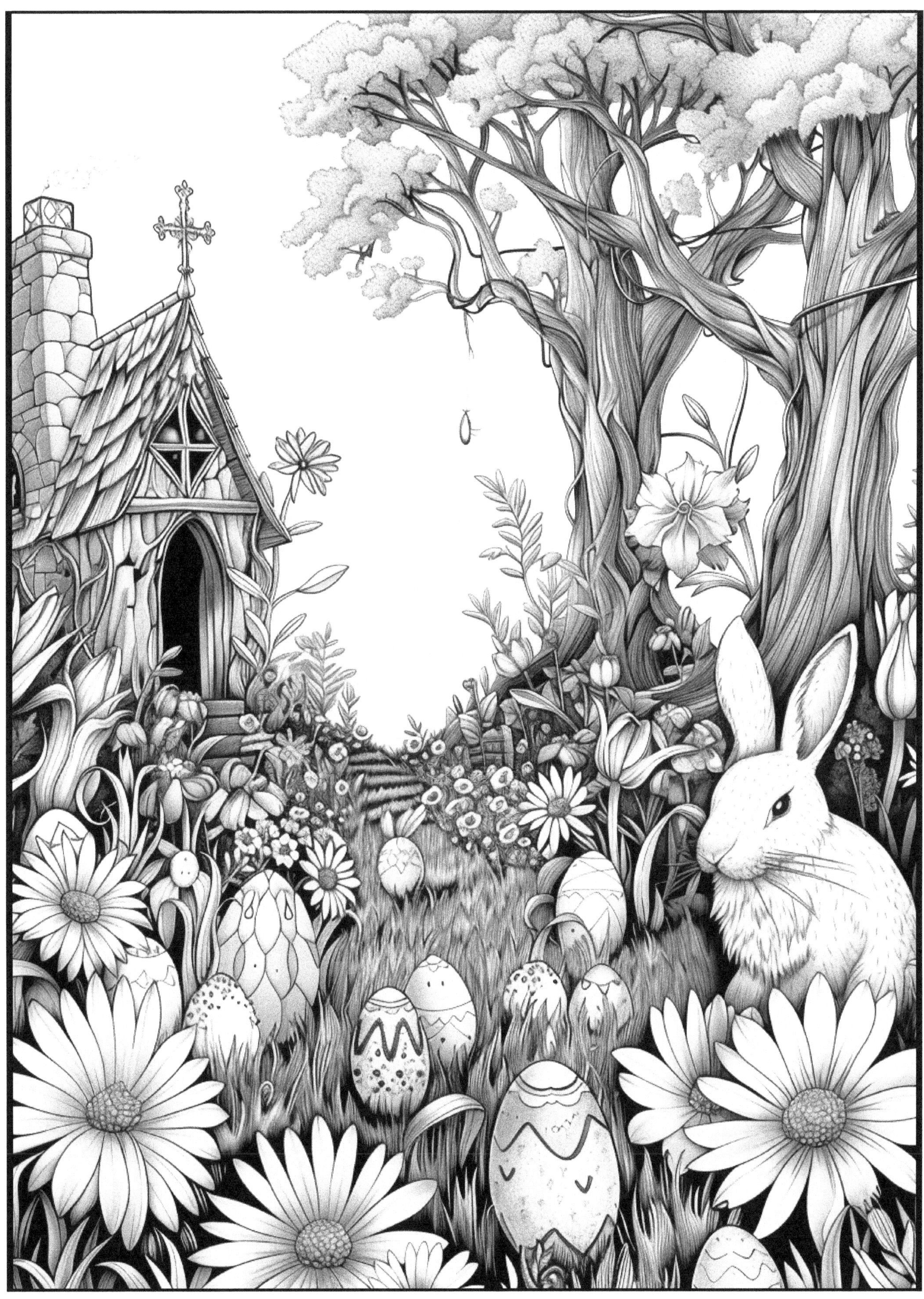

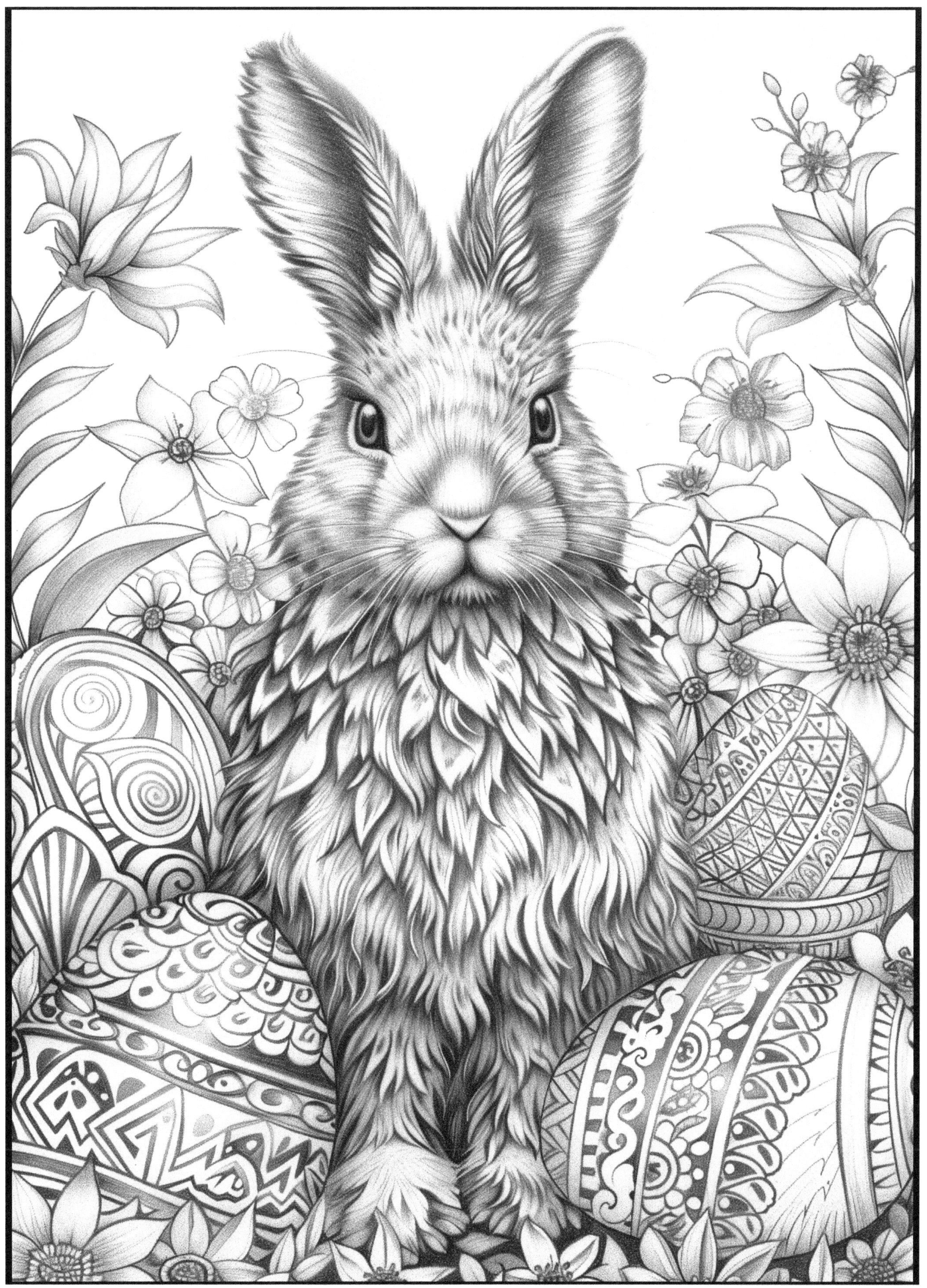

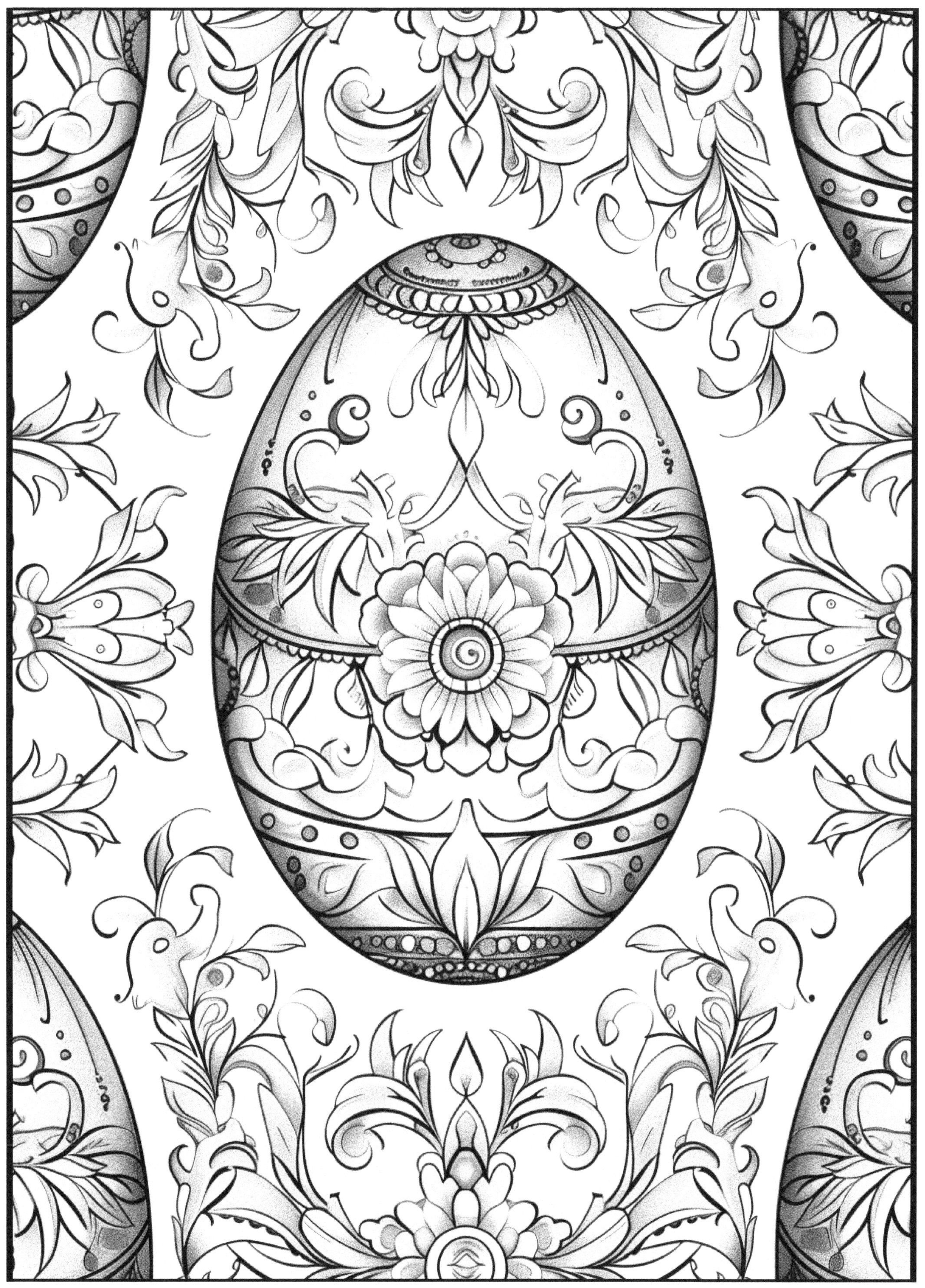

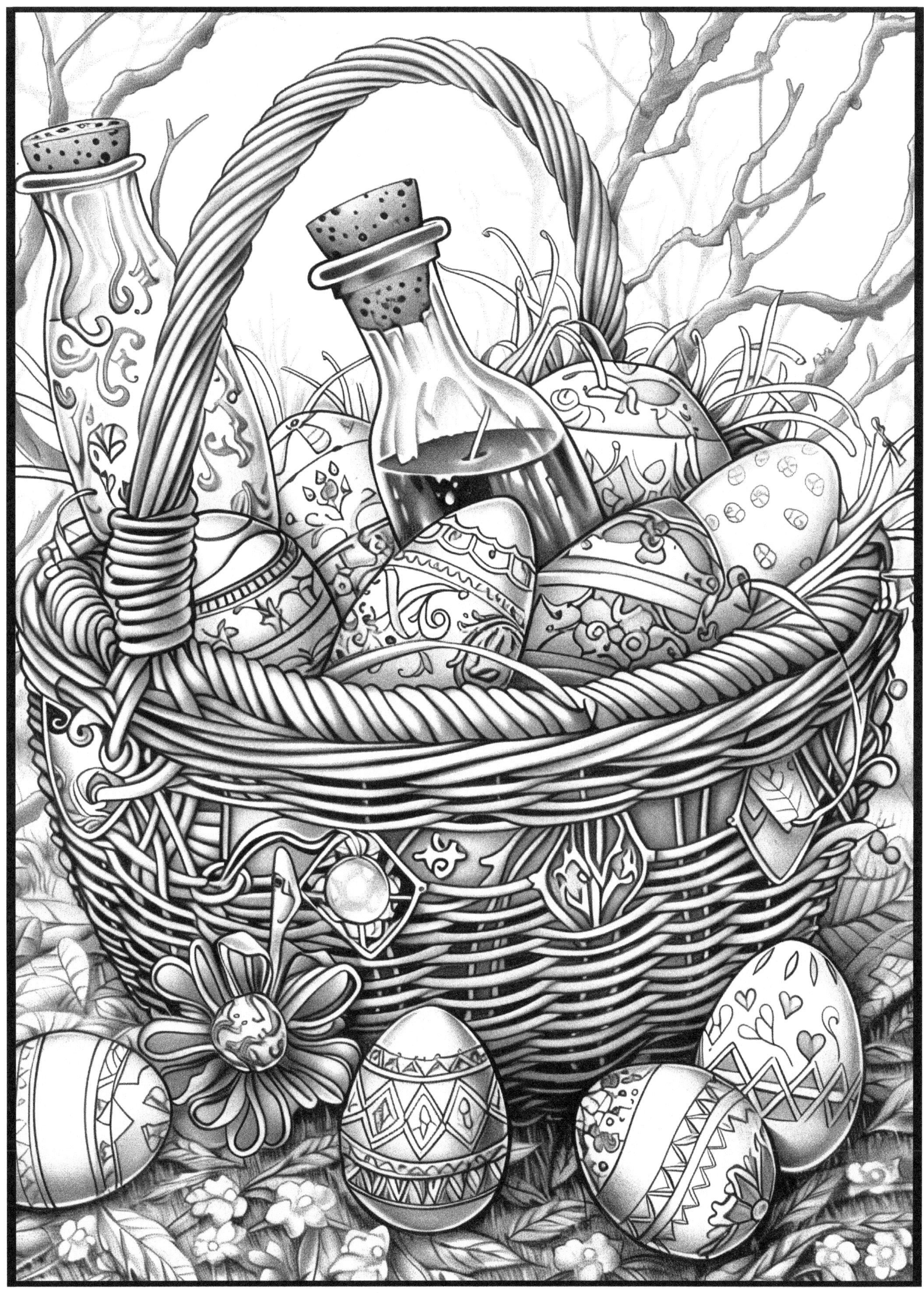

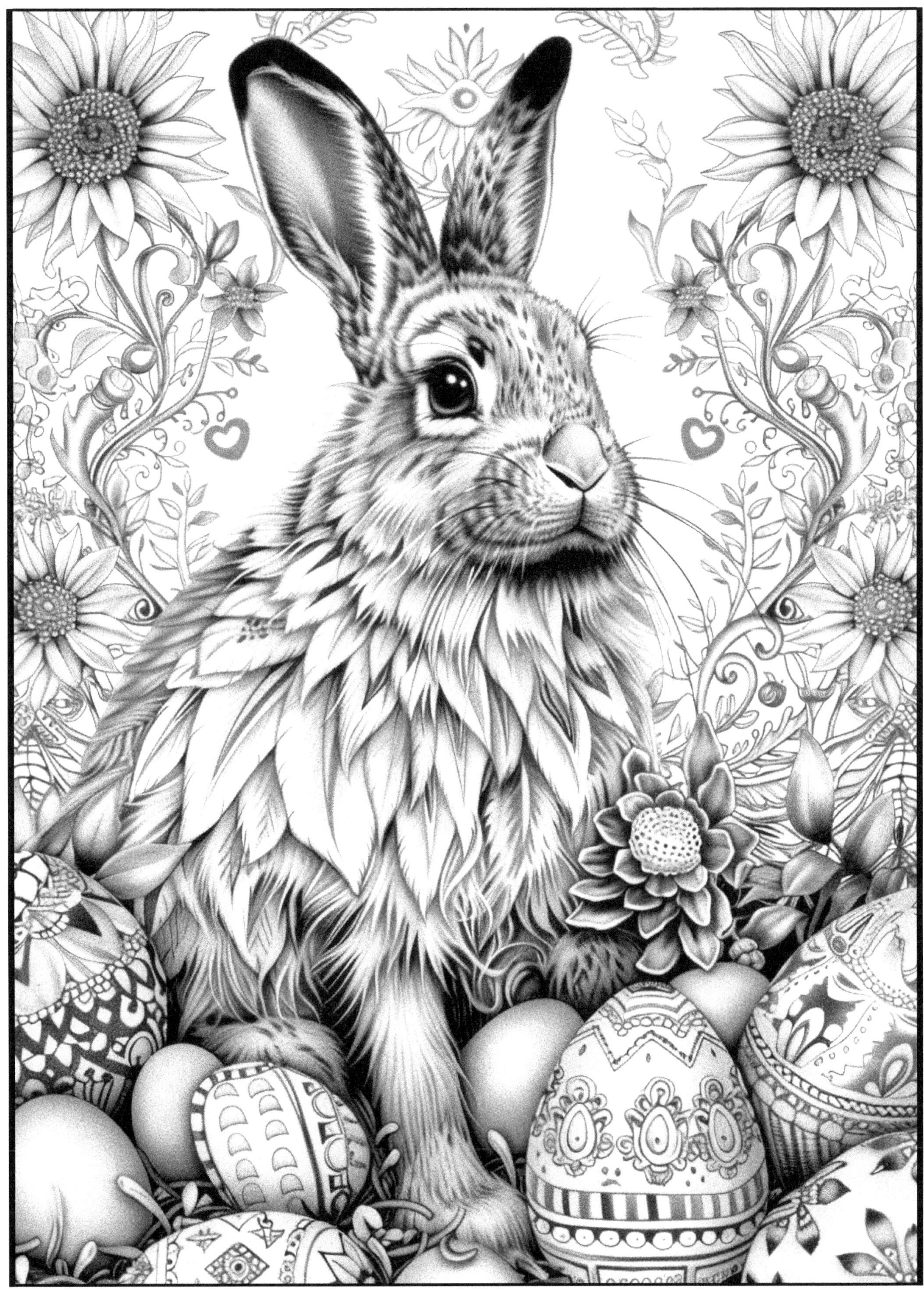

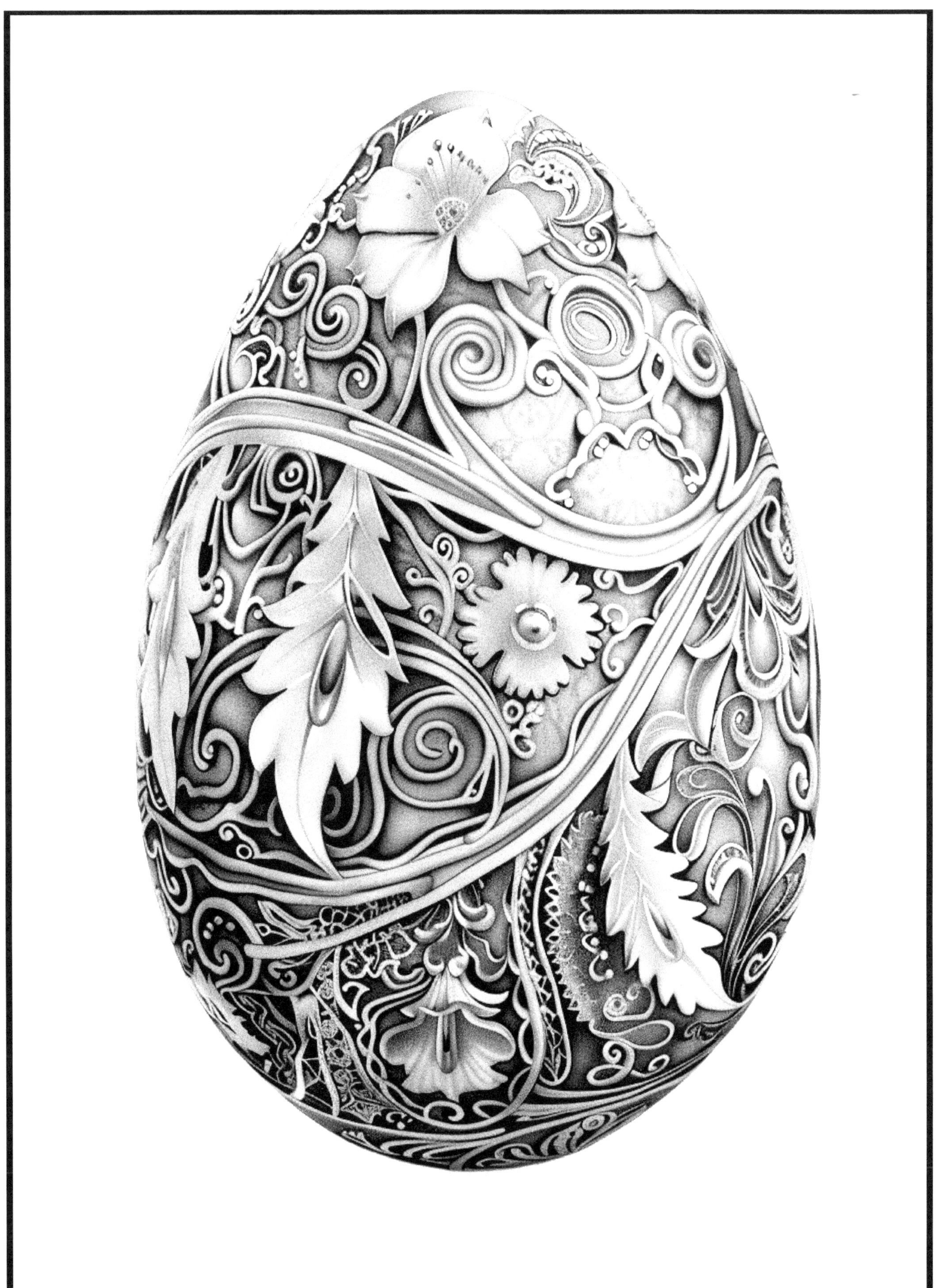

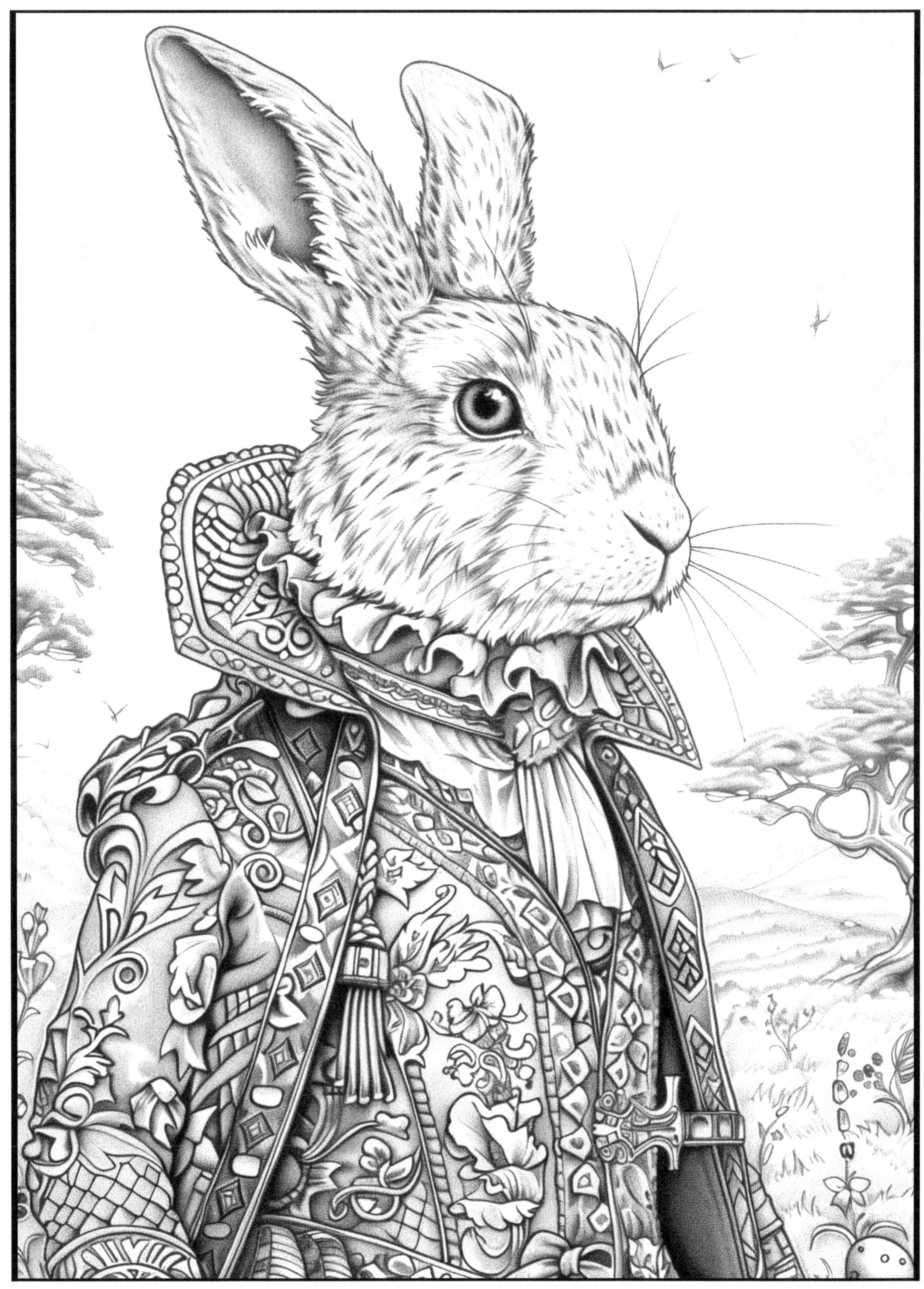

Your feedback is greatly appreciated!

It's through your feedback, support and reviews that we're able to create the best books possible and serve more people.

We would be extremely grateful if you could take just 60 seconds to kindly leave an honest review of the book on Amazon. Please share your feedback and thoughts for others to see.

To do so, simply find the book on Amazon's website (or wherever you purchased the book from) and locate the section to leave a review. Select a star rating and write a couple of sentences.

That's it! Thank you so much for your support.

Review this product

Share your thoughts with other customers

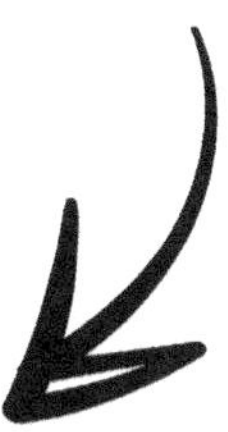

Write a customer review

www.ingramcontent.com/pod-product-compliance
Lightning Source LLC
LaVergne TN
LVHW081413110826
845149LV00010B/1735